The Ruby Savior

Love Amber,
I hope you
enjoy the
book

Love, Addison *

ADDISON HEFFERNAN

Paperback ISBN: 978-1-63616-131-0
eBook ISBN: 978-1-63616-132-7

Published By Opportune Independent Publishing Co.
www. opportunepublishing.com

Printed in the United States of America

For permission requests, please email the publisher with the subject
line as "Attention: Permissions Coordinator"
to the email address below:

Info@Opportunepublishing.com

TABLE OF CONTENTS

The Ruby Savior

Chapter One

Danielle Cayden was born to be a spy. She was a natural at blending in, fading into the background, and observing everything around her.

Dani was invisible and everyone knew it. She even knew it. But she didn't mind her role, in fact she valued it more than others may have thought.

Her mother and father had always said that she had been a quiet baby, never crying and being able to sleep through the night almost immediately after coming home from the hospital. She'd started walking at nine months and talking at nearly eleven.

While all other six year olds had been screaming and shouting on the playground Dani had been solemnly focused on climbing the monkey bars until she didn't fall into the mulch. When kids her age had been talking over each other in class Dani had been drawing silently or flipping through a chapter book untouched by the rest of her classmates.

Her parents called her mature. Grownups always said she had

impeccable manners and was the most polite young person they had ever met. Dani prided herself on that. Her power in life was being exceptionally ordinary and she relished it.

She wasn't popular and she never would be. Her grades were high enough to be proud of but didn't set any curves. She participated just enough to not warrant any unwanted attention from teachers. Dani was practical when it came to her work, getting as much done as she could during class so there was no homework left to do when she returned home.

In the grand scheme of things Dani was wallpaper.
Polite and personable wallpaper.

Her middle school was the type where there were so many kids that it was impossible to get through hallways without being packed like sardines. The noise level alone made staff shiver and wish they wore headphones.

Their last principal had made it a year before calling it quits and moving two cities away. The principal before that had made it three but was still receiving therapy for the torment he'd endured and now worked at a grocery store.

Considering the level of wilderness the school contained, it was only expected that a strict leader was desperately required to keep students in line and just months before Dani began attending, Margaret North had readily accepted the position.

Within Dani's first week of middle school Principal North had become feared by the entirety of the student population and deeply respected by the tired teachers and staff.

North's favorite pastime was giving speeches as frequently as the old loudspeaker would allow. It was an unfortunate hobby that led to her dispensing wisdom every morning to barely awake young teenagers.

In spite of herself, Dani still paid attention during morning announcements when her principal gave a two minute lecture about the importance of concentration a week before Thanksgiving break. The rest of the class either complained their way through it or simply pretended they couldn't hear anything at all.

That attitude continued into the entirety of English class as well.

"Do you have anything to contribute to our discussion, Danielle?" The English teacher was a stoic woman in her mid fifties who thought twelve and thirteen year olds were rude and annoying yet had taught them for nearly twenty years. Dani had been taking the class for months now and still didn't understand her teacher's career choice.

"No, thank you," She had been listening politely and attentively since class began. Dani was not the problem here and both she and her teacher were well aware of it. However being stared down by the class was most likely as much a highlight to her as it was a lowlight to Dani.

Mrs. Fredricks gave a curt nod. "Well then," she began, "please write the notes I've put on the board." The smirk on her face was barely hidden when the rows of students turned to stare at Dani at the back corner of the class.

"I already finished them." The reply had no hint of sarcasm in it but the teacher still looked offended. The class looked amused that the quiet girl had just made an adult speechless.

After that incident, Dani was not addressed for the rest of class just like always and the rest of her day passed just the same. Until and except for math.

Her final class of the day was one that Dani normally dreaded for all the usual reasons and then some. For starters, the classmates she had in math despised the subject more than she did and made their contempt for it known every minute the clock tucked closer to the end of class. None of the students were very nice to her either.

On the flip side, her math teacher was a jovial man named Mr. Stoop who had no stoop but wore tweed jackets with colorful patterned ties. He was entertaining at the very least.

Today there was a quiz, meaning Mr.Stoop was forced to be serious for forty five minutes, a rare occasion in itself. Nonetheless, Dani was greeted with a warm smile the second she passed through the door. "Good afternoon Dani,"

"Good afternoon," Stoop was the only one of her teachers who knew and used her preferred nickname just like he knew the names of every single other student who entered his room in the minutes following right up until the bell rang signaling the end of the passing period.

"Welcome in, welcome in everyone." Seventh period meant that all students were giddy to leave but still had just under an hour left. This time he was barely able to get their very much divided attention.

"Quiz today which as you all know you get all of class to complete. I wish you all the best of luck. Brendan, would you mind passing them out for me?" Mr. Stoop eyed a dark haired boy in the second row of desks.

Brendan was not someone Dani had ever talked to but from her observations he was popular, conceited, and obnoxious. Most of the time he was also half asleep.

"Of course, sir." Brendan was acting far too polite to not be suspicious and Dani would've bet her last dollar she knew the cause. The week prior he hadn't completed his work and had talked the entire class,interrupting the lesson. Mr. Stoop had threatened to bring him to the principal's office if he did it one more time.

He kept himself composed and quiet whilst passing out the sheets of paper, his small smile turning devilish when he reached the one Dani had been assigned. "No thank you for the messenger? I guess the cat still has your tongue, Cayden?" He snickered. "Just like always."

Dani glared, her eyes narrowed and teeth grinding together so hard dust almost formed. Comments like that usually didn't get under her skin nor did they warrant this much of a reaction from her. The sheer momentum of her anger made her hands feel strikingly hot, seething like she had caught them on fiery coals.

She nearly fell out of her chair when the reason was made clear, her brain disregarding everything and anything else.

Dani's hands weren't just searing hot, they were glowing bright red.

Chapter Two

"Is everything alright over there?" Mr. Stoop looked up from the stacks of papers strewn across his desk.

"Everything's fine, sir." Dani hoped that he believed it better than she did at the moment. Clearly if her hands were coated in a shimmering red and seething hot everything was not okay. They didn't hurt, but the dull tingling accompanying them made her hands feel like they were swarmed by ants.

Dani pinched herself carefully on the arm, frustrated when the only result was a faint pain. She definitely wasn't dreaming. Whatever had happened to her was real and it sent shivers down her spine.

There was no scientific explanation for why Dani's hands were warm and sparkly and that was enough to make her fall back in her chair once more. Before her brain could spiral she forced herself to focus back on the quiz where logic overruled everything else. Numbers made sense. The alternative didn't.

Dani finished her quiz in ten minutes, leaving her far too much time to attempt to act normal while staring at her now shaking hands. But first she let herself turn the quiz in, pulling the sleeves of her sweater over her hands so no one else could see them.

She'd made it five steps before her white sneakers were joined by a sleek black pair. "You look like you are going to be sick," their owner whispered. "Please just don't get your barf on my new shoes."

Dani looked up to see Brendan's smug face grinning at her menacingly. She glared. "Excuse me?" The harshness in her tone surprised her but Dani meant it all the same.

"Do you need to throw up your lunch?" Brendan inquired with mock politeness Dani wanted to roll her eyes at.

"No," She deadpanned, walking past him to the desk. It was unfortunate that he was faster on his feet. "Go away, please."

Only two more steps later they were approaching the desk where Mr. Stoop was doing a terrible job of pretending to not be listening. Dani beat Brendan, slamming her quiz down a split second before he could and then walking away just as fast.

A dull ache appeared in her head when she sat down, evidence of how awful Brendan truly was. Despite what she had promised now her stomach was starting to feel upset. Did she have a disease? Had she been poisoned? If that was the case, who had been the culprit?

Maybe her symptoms were thanks to Brendan's sickly smile he was throwing her way. Clearly he had noticed how pale Dani had gone because his new tactic involved pretending to retch over and over onto his desk.

A wave of anger flooding over her, all sense of respect leaving. "Leave. Me. Alone." Dani hissed,her hands coming in contact with the desk as she slapped her hands down. A shockwave of light appeared, red sparks spilling out in every direction and flying around the room like butterflies set free.

Students screamed. Brendan screamed. Stoop stood and looked right at her.

Her voice refused to work or form a coherent sentence. Her body refused to move.

Mr. Stoop, oddly enough, didn't seem disturbed in the slightest. "It's best we go now," He said, the urgency in his tone enough to snap her back to the present and get her legs to walk her right out of the door and to the hallway.

"What did I just do?" Dani barely registered saying the words. Everything in her felt frozen solid.

"You just manifested your power. Congratulations." Mr. Stoop kept a quick pace until the two of them reached the main hallway of the school. He kept his expression pleasant but refused to answer the questions Dani was now pummeling him with in rapid succession.

"My power?" She repeated for the third time. "What is that supposed to mean?"

Her teacher didn't answer, instead muttering words to himself so low that they were barely audible.

"Of course it had to manifest today." Mr. Stoop grumbled, his pleasant expression masking the emotion in his tone.

"You knew this was going to happen?" Dani was part walking and part jogging to keep up, coming to a screeching halt when her teacher stopped in front of a door Dani had never seen up close. He knocked.

"Can I help you?" Principal North stepped out of her office, her eyes on a folder she was holding. Dani shrunk back.

When her principal noticed who was watching her expression immediately changed to a look of concern. "Grennet, what's wrong?"

Dani was almost positive her teacher's first name was not Grennet.

"It happened," Mr Stoop moved Dani in between him and Principal North, blocking her exit. "And her sparks are even more powerful than we predicted."

Dani raised her hand. "Will someone please explain to me what's going on?" She didn't understand what the adults were talking about but none of it sounded good.

"Yes," Principal North agreed with a significant look at Mr. Stoop, leading them into the office.

"We can," Mr. Stoop moved forward,forcing Dani to follow her principal inside and take a seat behind the desk.

She held in a shiver when she saw him close the door and then lock it with them all inside.

Chapter Three

Sparks.

She had just shot sparks out of her hands.

That was somehow exhilarating.

But incredibly terrifying all the same.

And her teacher and principal both knew much more than they were letting on.

"So what is really going on?" Dani managed to not show how much fear was coursing through her, keeping her expression passive.

Principal North smiled pleasantly in return.

"It's nice to see you, Dani."

Dani hadn't known her principal knew her name.

"Um... hi," She managed weakly, ignoring her shaking hands to focus on the way her principal was staring at her now. Principal North was not the type for warm greetings but there she was, smiling at Dani like they were friends.

It was unnerving.

Mr. Stoop walked over and nudged her. "Giselle, she was a baby she won't remember us." His words seemed to help the principal reach an understanding and she nodded but that wasn't the only thing Dani latched onto.

"Isn't your first name Margaret?" Dani gestured to the framed diploma on the wall that said so. Her brain was spinning, trying to make sense of everything she had learned so far. A minute ago North had called Stoop Grennet and he had just called her Giselle. Those were names.

"It's best if we explain this very carefully." Mr. Stoop advised with a significant glance towards Principal North. His expression was worried and regretful, both making Dani's stomach churn with nerves.

"Okay," Dani had a sinking feeling this would not be a pleasant conversation for her.

"As I'm sure you've heard, what happened in the classroom was you manifesting your power." Principal North kept her hands neatly on the desk. "Right on time actually, you turned thirteen last week."

Dani nodded, too scared to ask how they had known her birthday was November Seventh.

"In Breckindale everyone is born with a power which reveals itself shortly after a brytlyn turns thirteen. It's a very big deal." "Breckindale?" That was all Dani could get in before her principal started speaking again. She needed to say something.

Anything.

"It's a realm separate from the one we are currently in," Mr. Stoop answered instead, his calm tone clearly for her benefit. "Your parents are it's rulers."

Dani's eyebrows raised so high they almost reached her hairline. "My parents are lawyers." Her parents were decently good at decision making but the idea of them ruling anything was laughable.

The adults exchanged another glance and Dani braced herself.

Principal North took a deep breath. "The people you live with are not your parents, Dani. We gave you to them when we brought you here as a baby." The woman's tone was gentle but her eyes were downcast.

Dani shook her head reflexively. "I've seen my baby pictures from the hospital right after I was born."

Giselle couldn't quite meet her eyes. "Those, I'm afraid we're created with magic. In order to give you the smoothest transition at only a few days old we altered the minds and memories of your human parents and a few others."

Mr Stoop took over, clearing his throat quietly. "Your biological parents are King Callan and Queen Amandine of Breckindale, making you a princess and second in line to the throne."

Dani's hands shook even more, the light from them illuminating her face in an eerie red glow. "I'm a princess?" The words wouldn't sink in. It had to be a cruel and brilliant joke.

"Correct," Principal North's nod was probably supposed to be reassuring but it did little to ease Dani's panic.

"And who are you two really?" The puzzle pieces Dani's head were starting to fit together into a puzzle she was forced to solve. She understood ~~enough to know~~ that the adults in front of her were most definitely not who they said they were.

"Our names are Grennet and Giselle. We are two of your parents advisors." Grennet extended a hand. Dani would have been proud of herself for her guess if her body didn't feel so numb.

Instead Dani gave a shaky breath and shook the offered hand. "Nice to meet you,"

The entire earth felt like it was crumbling around her one piece at a time. Lie after lie. Falling apart until Dani didn't see anything familiar.

"Are the children still in the classroom?" Giselle broke the suffocating silence and moved towards the door.

"I believe so, they were still there when we left." Grennet confirmed, the words so casual for such an intense situation.

Giselle nodded briskly. "Good, I'll handle that and then we can all head back."

"Head back where?" Dani latched on to the armrest of the chair until her shimmering knuckles were white under the red coating.

"Breckindale, of course." Giselle answered, her tone patient. "Now that you finally manifested, we can take you home."

If Giselle fully believed Dani considered Breckindale her home already she was very, very wrong.

Grennet waved his hand. "I'll get her ready, you go," He turned back to Dani the second Giselle closed the door.

"I apologize, she isn't usually this bossy. We've just been waiting anxiously for you to manifest and now that you have, there is a lot that must be put in order."

Dani folded her arms to her chest. "She's changing their memories isn't she? Just like my parents."

"Yes," Grennet answered, "and she'll do the same to the staff as well. Later on, some other Brytlyns will do a more thorough sweep." His words were too casual and made Dani uneasy. Was she really about to let two strangers take her to another realm?

"Did my real parents ask you to come get me?" She had to focus on other things. Things that didn't make her nauseous.

"Of course," Grennet took a silk pouch from his pocket. "They've been waiting a long time to be reunited with you again."

"What are they like?" Dani watched him empty the contents into his palm and unscrew the top of what appeared to be a glass perfume bottle.

"Callan and Amandine are wonderful,really. They are incredibly kind, good leaders too. You'll love them." He gave a grin and then chugged the liquid.

His skin smoothed itself out and his hair changed to a dark brown. He looked much younger, at least twenty five to thirty.

"You have a twin brother as well." He didn't miss a beat, paying no acknowledgment to the fact that he had become forty years younger in a few seconds.

"A twin brother?" Dani had never given a single thought to having a sibling. She'd been an only child her entire life.

"Wilfred," Grennet said, "He is older than you by four minutes which I'm sure he'll tell you. He's the heir to the throne. I think you'll like him."

Dani hoped so. Maybe having a twin would mean having her first friend ever.

"Is that what you really look like?" She asked.

"Yep," Grennet nodded, "I didn't really need a disguise anyway but I thought looking old would be funny." He put the empty bottle back into its pouch carefully as the door swung open.

"We can go now!" Giselle announced,striding into the room resolutely nodding.

Dani frowned. "Already? I thought you had to erase the whole school's memories."

"The team deployed to do that arrived a minute ago. Our priority right now is getting you out." Giselle explained, walking over to them.

"The sooner we get back the better," Grennet agreed.

Dani thought it best not to argue with the two adults. "How do we get to Breckindale?"

Grennet pulled out another silk pouch, this one a sapphire blue. "With these," He poured three diamonds into his palm and handed one to Giselle and the other to the skeptical girl still in her chair.

Giselle gave a kind smile when she noticed Dani's hesitation. "Just imagine the place you want to go in your head and crush the gemstone."

Dani narrowed her eyes. "Crush it?" There was no way. "As in smash into tiny pieces?"

Giselle nodded. "Grennet,why don't you blink and show her."
"Blink?" Dani slowly stood from her chair, her hands still warm and shimmery with red.

Giselle shot Grennet an amused look and moved to Dani's side. "I'm sorry Dani, blinking is what humans would probably call teleporting."

"Oh," In a weird and twisted way that made sense to Dani. She couldn't tell if that was relieving or terrifying.

"Watch me," Grennet instructed, holding his hand out in front of him, the Diamond in the center of his palm. He closed his eyes,curled his fingers inward, and disappeared in a flash of white light a second later.

Dani couldn't keep her jaw from dropping nor her eyes to focus on anything but the spot Grennet had been standing right before.

"Your turn,Dani." Giselle mimed the motion Grennet had done and waited for Dani to follow suit.

Dani didn't budge. "So I just crush it and think of what?"

"Elthorne Palace," Giselle gave her the location. "Your family is waiting for you there."

"I live in a palace." Dani mumbled the words mostly for herself but Giselle nodded anyway,another amused smile playing on her lips

"You live in a palace," Giselle agreed,miming the motions again.

This time Dani obliged, holding her shimmering right hand out, closing her eyes tightly, and saying the words over and over in her head until a breeze whipped through her hair and light overtook every sense.

And then Dani left earth for the final time.

Chapter Four

"I really get to live here?" Dani couldn't help staring at the enormous cream castle stretching as tall and wide as she could see.

"Did you think we were kidding about your family being royal?" Grennet smiled broadly. Since their arrival he had switched his teacher disguise for a hunter green tunic and pants.

Dani's eyes were as wide as they could go. "I believed you," She mumbled,craning her neck to see the top of the highest tower that was mostly covered by wispy clouds.

Everything in Breckindale was bright but muted in pastels. The air was fresh and clear with the purest green trees and shrubbery Dani had ever laid eyes on.

"Welcome to Elthorne Palace." Giselle spun around to face them. Her strawberry blond hair fell in soft curls down the back of her pink gown adorned with what Dani was positive were genuine pearls.

They paused at the iron and golden furnished gates that stood at the end of the path. Guards were stationed beside two posts,both of whom saluted when they saw the group and waved them through the opening gates. Inside was a courtyard filled with the vibrant green grass surrounding a winding path of stone.

A few yards up a fountain sat, polished cream stone with gold on the edges, leading further up the path to where a dozen more guards were stationed white uniforms perfectly pressed. When Grennet and Giselle reached them they all saluted. When Dani joined them a step later they bowed.

It made her feel about as conspicuous as if her hair was suddenly as bright as the grass.

"Your royal highness," a guard with dark skin and a uniform almost completely covered in medals moved forward to greet her. "Welcome home."

Dani managed an uneasy smile. "Thank you," She was grateful her manners had stayed intact while the rest of her was in shock. Grennet and Giselle had to move her forward as more guards saluted and opened the double doors for them.

"This is incredible!" She breathed,eyes even wider trying to take in the whole foyer at once.

The floor was pure white and golden marble with high arched ceilings and a staircase in the center that could fit at least fifteen people across every step. A crystal chandelier hung from the ceiling, casting specks of light across the walls.

Dani was only aware that she wasn't dreaming because Grennet kept nudging her. There was even gold filigree climbing the walls just like the outside.

A large balcony made of the same gold as the staircase railings seemed to span the entirety of the second floor, ending only where the stairs led. Three people were headed straight for that landing and they all shared the same dark hair and pale complexion Dani did.

One was a tall man in what appeared to be halfway between a suit and a uniform adorned with medals and sashes in jeweled tones. Callan had brown hair the same exact shade of Dani's and a neatly trimmed mustache and beard. He walked with purpose, deep in conversation with the woman beside him.

Amandine wore a pale yellow gown and had dark curls rippling down her back. Even from so far below Dani could see the diamonds on her earrings and necklace, sparking in the light. She looked impossibly regal, even just walking down a hallway in her own home.

Behind them was a young teenager with the same hair as his father but a shade lighter than his mother. Wilfred wore a dark blue blazer over a collared shirt with matching pants and shoes. He was taller than Dani but only by an inch or two and from what she could see of his features they were a perfect match for hers.

He was also the one who noticed her first. His vivid green eyes meeting hers from above.

Dani considered herself decently good at sports but there was no way she could have side stepped Callan and Amandine the way her twin brother had, bounding down the stairs two at a time while still managing to look composed.

He joined them in the center of the foyer, grinning at Dani. "So you must be my long lost twin sister."

"I'm Danielle," She said.

Her brother nodded. "But you go by your nickname too right? That's what mom and dad said." He gestured back to Callan and Amandine who were now descending the staircase.

"Dani," She replied, "I go by Dani."

"I go by Will," her brother added. "Wilfred is a mouthful."

Dani nodded her agreement.

"Unfortunately Grennet, Giselle, and the rest of the Magicals still use my full name." He suppressed another grin as he zeroed in on the advisors flanking Dani.

Giselle smiled patiently, clearly having heard the complaint before. "It's your proper name."

"You don't call me Danielle though." Dani piped up, turning

to Giselle with an expression identical to Will's.

Giselle stayed unruffled. "Because you aren't the heir to the throne,"

Will looked like he wanted to protest further but sighed instead. "That's fair," By the time his frown went right back to a smile their parents were beside him,eyes brimming with tears.

"Hello darling," Amandine's voice was thick with emotion now and she was close enough for Dani to fully grasp how similar the two of them truly were. Same arched eyebrows, eye shape, lips, even the smile lines her mom was now displaying. Dani's eye color and nose were all from her father.

Dani had resembled her human parents close enough for no questions to be posed on if she was truly their daughter but compared to how close she resembled the adults in front of her the humans might as well have been randomly selected strangers. She was a miniature version of Amandine with flecks of Callan. A perfect match.

Her hands started shaking again, heat swarming through her like bottled up lightning.

Breathe Dani.

A voice identical to Giselle's flooded her senses like an echo of a memory. When she turned to check, however, Giselle most definitely wasn't saying anything. She wasn't even looking in Dani's direction instead in deep conversation with Amandine.

"What was that?" Dani's brain was spinning trying to find a logical explanation. The only one she could come up with made her insides crawl. In Breckindale everyone had a magic power. One of the most popular ones in movies was telepathy.

Giselle turned to face her. "Sorry, I just wanted to see if my power would work now that we are back." She said the words out loud this time, her tone apologetic.

And you looked a little overwhelmed.

That last part hadn't been.

Dani's eyes grew wide,hands shaking. "That's your power isn't it?"

Giselle nodded. "I'm a transferer just like Wilfred," If she saw Will grimace she paid him no mind, instead brightening her smile. "I can transfer messages into other's heads and read minds."

It's not as creepy as it sounds

Evidently, Giselle had been reading Dani's last few thoughts.

"Does everyone have a different power here?" Dani wondered, hoping for an answer that didn't come through as a weird echo.

Her twin brother shrugged. "There are lots of different kinds," he told her. "Being a transferer is pretty cool though."

Dani wasn't sure that having a twin brother who could read her mind all the time was a good thing.

The only thing she was sure of was that Breckindale was a very odd place. But somehow it already felt a little like home.

Chapter Five

Giselle and Grennet left shortly after that, chatting with Callan and Amandine briefly before blinking away and leaving Dani alone with her family. She wasn't quite sure how to feel about that.

In truth, Dani was still in shock over the whole situation. It didn't feel real: the palace, the family, the title, any of it.

The first stop of her tour of Elthorne was to see her bedroom which Dani nearly fainted at the sight of. Her room was not only giant but exquisite with a four poster bed, a complete wall of glass windows, a ceiling covered in a stunning mural of a bright blue sky, and rose gold statues and filigree curling down her bed posts and walls. It was fit for a princess and Dani just couldn't believe that princess was her.

Her disbelief only grew when she was introduced to her bodyguard, the same guard who had welcomed her to Elthorne not even half an hour before. Lieutenant Anders Bower would accompany her everywhere on and off palace grounds for security purposes. Once Will clarified he and their parents all had bodyguards Dani felt less terrified at the prospect.

With Anders in tow, Dani was introduced to the palace staff, everyone from the head cook Ms. Lannister to the head of security Colonel Karcher Jesclen. Per the requests of their parents, all staff at Elthorne was supposed to call Dani and Will by their first names.

"There are a lot of people here," Dani noted, walking beside her brother as they followed their parents through a miniature art gallery displaying dozens of portraits.

"We have a huge staff," Will agreed, "I guess having such a big palace warrants it."

Dani stared at a portrait of a different palace, one with dark stone and no towers. "Seems logical,"

"The royal family had lived in Elthorne Palace for hundreds of years without fail. It's taken over by the heir to the throne when he or she assumes the throne." Will explained, examining a sculpture of a knight.

Dani was second in line to the throne not first. "So you'll live here when you become king?"

Will nodded. "Though I guess if you wanted it you could stay here too."

"It is a really cool palace," Dani agreed.

Her twin's grin turned mischievous. "And you haven't even seen all of the secret passages yet. The whole palace is littered with them."

"I'm guessing that won't be a part of this tour?"

Her brother laughed. "I'll show you them tomorrow. It'll be nice having someone to explore with now that you're here."

"Yeah, it will." Dani replied. Her brother was friendly and he genuinely wanted to talk to her, a big change from the kids she'd gone to school with on earth.

"I still can't believe you're actually here. Mom and dad said it would be soon since I manifested the day after our birthday and twins usually manifest close together. Though I guess since you already manifested once so the system got messed up."

Dani stopped him. "I already manifested?" She had only heard that she had manifested earlier. Never before that. Surely she would've remembered manifesting the first time if the second was so ingrained in her memory.

Will's smile disappeared. "It happened right after we were born. It wasn't supposed to happen."

"Explain," Dani told him,crossing her arms as they reached the next hall.

"I don't know how much Giselle and Grennet told you about powers but they only reveal themselves after thirteenth birthdays because that's when our bodies are fully ready to accept that amount of magic. Baby's bodies are definitely not ready for such a large amount of magic so young so mom told me that after you manifested you had to be taken to a realm where your magic could dull and not kill you from the inside out."

Dani hadn't known any of that. Giselle had explained that she had been brought to earth as a baby but that was the full extent of Dani's knowledge on the subject. She couldn't decide if the explanation had made her feel better or worse but she knew something still didn't fit.

"I didn't feel any different on earth before I manifested today. Wouldn't I have felt something?"

Will considered this and shrugged. "I'm not sure, this is the first time something like that has happened, I think. Maybe you can ask Cornelius when he comes tomorrow."

Dani had been told early on in the tour that Cornelius was the royal physician and that he would be coming the next day to purge her of the toxins living on earth had given her.

"Anything else I should know about Breckindale?" She asked, smiling until her twin regained his own.

Will cleared his throat and straightened his back, clearly imitating someone else. "Breckindale is a magical realm that exists separately from all others but on the same timeline. King Callan and Queen Amandine have been ruling for twenty years with the ruling council of Magicals as their advisors."

"Hold up. Mom and dad have been ruling for twenty years?" They only looked to be in their thirties themselves, far younger than Dani had imagined.

"Brytlyns bodies start aging slower when we turn twenty one thanks to the magic in us. It preserves us far longer than humans are able to live I'm sure."

"That's strange."

"To you maybe, you've been living with them your whole life."

"True,"

"So, how are you taking all of this?" Will veered left, following the route their parents were taking. "I'm sure it's a lot."

"It is," Dani agreed. "But I really like it here so far."

Old Dani had been fine with blending into the background and being silent while the world moved on around her. New Dani lived in a shimmering palace and had a personal staff at her beck and call for every request. It was a lot for her tangled knot of emotions to digest.

When her twin brother nodded, Dani couldn't tell if he had been inside her mind. "Well I for one am very glad that we're finally reunited. And I promise I won't prank you while you are sleeping." The last part was said so solemnly Dani almost laughed.

"I'd appreciate it," She grinned when he did.

The rest of the tour was easy enough to pay attention to thanks to having Will as company and plenty to look at. Dinner was the only time that homesickness set in, though Will's jovial conversation kept her from thinking about it too much.

In her head, Dani knew she shouldn't miss the humans that had raised her but her heart didn't get the memo at all. Every happy memory had taken place with the two of them and sitting so close to the people they had been chosen to replace was harder than she wanted to admit.

Lying in her new bed, in her new room, in her new palace, in her new realm Dani couldn't help but reflect on everything she'd gone through. The life she knew had been flipped on its head and turned bright and sparkly.

Everything had changed but the girl in the middle of this mess. The same girl who was trying to focus on every single positive instead of all the negatives.

Here she mattered. Dani had the best opportunity possible to break out of her shadow she'd been in for so long: the invisible girl. She was a princess now, a princess with odds stacked all in her favor.

And somehow, that thought was enough to ease her into sleep.

Chapter Six

"You think I should keep my power a secret?"

Dani placed her fork down on her plate and stared across the golden rimmed table at her father. She had been told during dinner the previous day that breakfast was served in the formal dining room of Elthorne every morning at about seven.

"Just for now until you are fully acclimated. Brytlyns will ask questions, they always do, and it would be best for those questions to be asked later on." Callan explained carefully.

Dani shrugged, lifting her fork back up and spearing a piece of fruit. "Fine by me," The less people who knew about her power,the better she would be able to fit in.

Amandine nodded, her smile approving. "Now that that's settled we can move onto our next order of business."

"What's that?" Dani wondered, sweeping her hair off of the shoulder of her new lavender gown, identical in every way but color to the dozens more hanging in her closet.

Less than twenty four hours of being in Breckindale and her royal makeover had already begun. Her new look included pastel dresses, gemstone flats, and dainty jewelry with pearls and diamonds. Now that she had an entire realm to represent brushing through her hair once and washing her face wasn't going to cut it.

"Your enrollment at Crystalium Academy."

Dani furrowed her brows. "Crystalium?" She repeated, the words unfamiliar on her tongue.

"It's the school Will attends and we think it may be a good fit for you as well," Callan explained, glancing at his son beside him.

"You'll love it," Her brother promised, nodding earnestly.

Dani narrowed her eyes cautiously. "Are brytlyn schools different than human ones?" Considering what Dani had seen of the realm so far she was positive the answer was yes.

But Callan shook his head. "From the reports we received from Grennet and Giselle there isn't much difference except for the structure and subjects of the classes."

"At Crystalium we are each put into a pod of about thirty kids in our grade and go to all your classes together minus training sessions. Our physical education sessions too, but the entire grade has that all together so it doesn't really count." Will explained, fidgeting with the sleeve of his dark blue blazer.

Dani nodded, that didn't sound so bad. "How many classes do we have a day?"

"Two every day but we spend three hours in each class." He mumbled through a mouthful.

"Because we only take that class once a week." Dani guessed, earning impressed nods from her parents.

Will pointed his fork at her. "Bingo," He said.

"When would I start?" She turned away from her brother to glance at her mom and dad.

"Monday at the earliest," Callan said, quickly glancing at Amandine. "We are meeting with the headmistress later today to discuss it."

Three days. In three days she would be sent into the magical lion's den.

"I thought you were meeting with the Magicals today?" Will piped up, pushing his plate away and folding his napkin beside it.

"In half an hour," Callan confirmed, switching his gaze from one twin to the other. "They will be releasing the notice of your return to the public today."

Dani twisted her fingers in her napkin. "What are they going to say?"

She wasn't sure there was an easy way to explain her hurried return while neglecting the power that had led to it.

Will met her eyes, shrugging carelessly. "I'm sure they'll figure out something,"

It took Dani a moment to realize he must have used his power to see her thoughts. It took one more for her mother to react.

"Will," Amandine intoned quietly, giving him a stern look that even made Dani shrink back.

"Sorry," Will apologized to their mother first before turning to Dani. "Sorry,"

"It's okay," Dani wasn't a big fan of having her thoughts prodded by her twin. no more than she enjoyed shooting sparks around rooms. She shook the memory away as quickly as it had come. "What time is Cornelius coming?"

"Around eleven was what he told me." Callan answered, finishing his plate just as staff came to clear them all away. Just like the rest of her family, she thanked them and then left for the foyer.

Amandine and Callan had to go prepare for their meeting and Will was being forced to attend school so after some hugs and reluctant goodbyes Dani was left alone in the foyer with her bodyguard.

Anders narrowed his eyes on her. "Are you alright? You've

been standing in the same spot and staring at the doors for five minutes."

"I'm just trying to figure out what to do until my appointment." The possibilities in Elthorne were endless and dizzying.

"What interests you?"

Dani's mind immediately went to drawing and reading, remembering the gigantic library she had seen the day before. It had to have been filled with thousands of books.

"Reading," But as much as Dani would have loved to spend hours scouring the shelves upstairs, another idea piqued her interest more. "Actually Anders, is there anything here about my family?"

Her bodyguard looked confused. "Pardon?"

"I want to learn more about my family history," Anything at all would have been a decent start.

Her bodyguard nodded once. "Follow me," He led the way through a hall near the front of the palace, stopping at each room and playing tour guide.

The first room was just a drawing room with baby blue walls and cream sofas on either side of a small table. Further down there was a small ballroom, what Anders explained to be staff quarters, a parlor, and a coat closet.

The final room in the corridor was a library only a fourth of the size of the larger one upstairs. This one held only one wall of shelves containing volumes with yellowed pages and leather covers.

"Family records," Anders explained, "Photo albums, old journals."

Dani carefully took out a violet covered book with precise gold lettering. "Quite a family history," She mumbled.

"Incredibly extensive," Her guard agreed. "You'll learn more about it at Crystalium but your lineage has been carefully curated for centuries."

Dani plopped down on the nearest sofa, opening the large volume and flipping through the ancient pages. The book appeared to be an overview of the royal family from two hundred years before. Just what she needed.

She flipped to a portrait of four people, each clad in regal outfits and jewels. "King Redger and Queen Eliza with Crown Prince Bren and Princess Delacour." Dani read the caption aloud.

"Crown Prince Bren was your father's great grandfather," Anders noticed from his position at the door. He managed to keep an eye on the exit and her at all times.

Dani had to admit her father and Bren shared a decent resemblance as did the old crown prince and the current one.

Even Dani saw a bit of herself in Delacour, standing beside her older brother looking serene and proud.

She was still staring at the portrait when multiple voices echoed in from the foyer, some male and some female.

"The Magicals?" Dani looked up at an undisturbed Anders. It had been at least half an hour since breakfast ended.

Before he could answer, a tall woman in a dark uniform entered and looked Dani straight in the eye. "I apologize for the interruption but the King and Queen have requested you meet them in the foyer to be introduced to their guests." That was all she said,turning back on her heel and walking away before Dani had a chance to respond.

She had said guests, and it was far too early for Cornelius to be arriving. It had to be the Magicals! Callan and Amandine wanted her to meet their advisors, the people who had chosen who would raise her on earth and brought her there.

She jumped out of her seat, leaving her book on the sofa and followed Anders out of the library.

Chapter Seven

By the time Dani and Anders made it to the foyer her parents were standing with eight other adults Grennet and Giselle included.

Dani moved to stand beside Callan and Amandine who both gave warm smiles and beckoned her over. Anders stood near the grand staircase, assessing the scene silently.

Callan put a hand on her shoulder, steering her forward to face the Magicals. "Dani, I want you to meet Edon, Cordelia, Arabella, Ronan, Iris, and Milos. You already know Giselle and Grennet." He pointed to each in turn when he said their names.

"Hello," Dani replied, trying not to shrink under the gazes of so many people.

"She's certainly grown," Cordelia smiled, smoothing her long dark braids with a delicate hand, leaving them to fall down to the bodice of her pale green gown.

"The twins turned thirteen last week," Giselle reminded her, looking utterly regal in an amber gown and intricate braided bun. She gave Dani a quick wave.

How are you settling in?

Dani resisted the urge to shiver when the message came through, the words just as hollow and creepy as before. Instead she focused all her energy in sending back a response.

Good so far. I like it here.

Dani repeated the thought a few times for good measure until Giselle nodded, confirming she'd seen the thought. She still had loads of questions about how transfering worked but now wasn't a great time to ask.

"We are all glad you made it back safely." Edon's thick black hair bounced slightly when he spoke, his words precise but kind.

"As I'm sure you realized the plan changed quite suddenly before your departure." Ronan's skin was the same color as his pale blond hair but his eyes were steel gray. His expression was calm.

None of us expected you to manifest yesterday so leaving became something of a scramble once we had to deal with the class of humans and such.

Giselle's eyes were on Milos and Arabella while they spoke to

Dani's parents but her message came through loud and clear.

Will said that was the second time that I manifested.

Dani couldn't help but stare at Giselle as she repeated her answer over and over in her head. Unfortunately before Giselle sent a response a Magical with long dark hair, impossibly pink cheeks, and red lips spoke up.

"Congratulations on manifesting yesterday,Danielle. That is always such a special moment for any young brytlyn." Iris said the words with such sweetness that it was hard to tell if she was being genuine. Dani had caught her glaring at her a moment before so she figured it wasn't.

"Thank you," Dani gave a small smile in return. Polite. Unassuming. Careful.

Wilfred wasn't incorrect about you manifesting once before. You manifested shortly after your birth and in order to save you from your power we had to take you to a realm where it wouldn't cause you any harm. All of us were involved in the decision but only a few of us were present to see you manifest.

Giselle managed to not look at her during her explanation but Dani couldn't even pretend to focus on anything else. Will had given a similar explanation the day before but having it confirmed by someone behind the decision made it feel that much more real and at least twenty times as painful.

Dani had been born in Breckindale thirteen years before and

been taken away just as fast and given to two humans to raise as their own with no clues as to where she was truly from. It was difficult to think about.

When a voice brought her back to the less painful present Dani was all too thankful.

"Yes, from what Giselle and Grennet have told us, you have a very interesting power indeed." Milos was on the shorter side with brown hair, tan skin, and a broad grin.

"Dani's a sparker," Amandine answered, placing a comforting hand on her arm.

Arabella nodded, glancing at Milos. "It's a very rare power as well."

Dani perked up. "It's rare?" In a realm full of people with magic she had assumed there had to be dozens of others who could create sparks just like hers.

"There is only one other sparker currently alive," Callan told her, his tone calm but jaw tight. Clearly her father was either bothered by the question or simply didn't like his answer. Dani wondered if her power was just a sore spot in general.

"I'm sure you love your power don't you?" Iris spoke to Dani like she was a small child in need of coddling. "Sparks can be a beautiful thing when controlled."

If someone had been holding a microphone it would have

been dropped and giving out static at that moment.

Giselle stared at Iris like the other Magical had just murdered her favorite puppy. Grennet looked annoyed. Arabella pressed her lips into a thin line. They all stared at Iris but spoke no words, the silence an answer in itself.

"I heard you enjoy reading?" Arabella smoothly changed the subject to something that didn't make Dani's brain work overtime trying to translate.

"Yes," Dani replied. Reading had given her a way out that didn't make her feel invisible at school.

Arabella looked genuinely interested at her answer, the exact opposite of Iris who seemed offended that Dani liked books.

Giselle noticed and glared. Arabella didn't. "What's your favorite genre?"

"Non fiction, I guess, but I started reading some fantasy this year." Her life was a fantasy book now, a very odd notion indeed.

Grennet grinned proudly. "Told you she came prepared," The other Magicals nodded attentively, everyone except Iris who was now picking at her nails.

His words solidified something for her. "You were the one who suggested I start reading those," She realized,eyes wide with recognition. "You told me they were interesting reads and worth a try."

Grennet just grinned. "I thought it might be good for you to get a taste of what Breckindale would be like before you came." Dani suspected his assumption was correct.

"How long have you been preparing me for this?" She expanded her gaze to take in all of the Magicals, since they had all clearly played a part.

"A while now," Dani had expected Giselle or Grennet to answer but the sugary tone was all Iris.

"You have to be ready for whatever future lies ahead of you." Giselle clarified, shooting Iris a warning look the other Magical was ignoring.

Instead Iris just gave Dani a sparkling smile.
"If it isn't chosen already."

Chapter Eight

What does she mean?

Dani stared straight at Giselle, only vaguely aware of Callan pulling her closer and Amandine's grip on her arm tightening.

"I believe Dani has to go get ready for her appointment now." Amandine announced, sounding perfectly natural while lying through her teeth.

Callan gave her a look and Dani had the good sense not to contradict them, following her head of security up the grand staircase without as much as a goodbye to the Magicals.

"Do you know what that was about?" Dani waited until they were past the landing and well out of earshot before turning to Anders. "What Iris just said."

And what Giselle hadn't.

"High Councilor Iris has always been one of the most outspoken members out of your parents council."

Dani didn't doubt that. "I think she was egging me on with her manifesting comments,"

"Perhaps," Anders signaled to the guards on either side of the library doors to let them in. Both of them bowed when Dani walked in after her guard.

"And her last bit could have been a warning," Dani added. "Or maybe it was a threat?"

"I would like to think Iris would not choose to threaten you." Anders scanned the whole room in less than three seconds. "However, if you legitimately do feel threatened I will speak with her and the situation will be handled."

That was her life now, one word and everything would be handled. "No thank you," That promise legitimately sounded like a threat in itself.

"Fair enough, but if you do ever feel threatened or in danger it is my job to take care of it."
"Does that happen often?"
"Being threatened or in danger?"

Dani had seen the guards stationed all over Elthorne and its grounds. She knew how protected she was.

"Your family happens to be very popular with the public but there are of course bound to be some outliers among the realm's citizens. "Anders added no emphasis to his implications, stating them as plainly as humans would state the weather.

Dani nodded as calmly as she could. "Do you think I will be threatened?" She hadn't considered ever being in danger in a realm that looked so calm and picturesque. Looks could be deceiving.

Anders kept his expression passive. "I think people do not like what they cannot understand and once the statement of your arrival has been released and rumors start circulating of the circumstances it could be a possibility."

Dani let the statement sink in.

"None of this is meant to scare you, however, I believe it best that you gain some understanding of why you are given so much security. You may not be directly in line for the throne but you will need to be protected for the rest of your life."

"Right, I'm not the heir so shouldn't my brother be in more danger then I am?" Monarchs and their heirs were usually the ones blame was placed on in an event of outrage, not the princess who just happened to have lived a crazy childhood.

Anders shook his head once. "In normal circumstances I would not hesitate to say yes. These are not normal circumstances."

"So it isn't normal for a long lost princess to come back after thirteen years because her power isn't trying to kill her anymore?" Dani had only been half kidding. "Besides, how much could my arrival have changed?"

"There is no telling how the public will react," Anders stated calmly.

Naturally, Dani's vivid imagination spawned terrifying images that involved pitchforks, fire, and a place coup intent on exiling the dangerous monster hiding inside the cream walls. The monster then watched helplessly from an arched window as her sparks whipped around the fake crowd and reined their terror against the mob.

Dani blinked the future nightmares away and ignored her now shimmering hands. "I don't want to change things. I don't want to get threatened." Dani didn't want any of this.

Anders' gaze softened for a moment. "I know you don't, and that's why I am here."

The silence that followed was deafening but the silence made Dani feel better, if only slightly.

She was protected here.
She had a bodyguard.
She wasn't a monster.

"Anders, can I ask you a question?" She moved towards one of the shelves.

"What's on your mind?"
"If I won't be queen when I'm older, what is my role?"

"You'll have the freedom to choose that for yourself in the future. For now I suggest you focus on getting acclimated to

Breckindale and eventually on your studies."

"Good point," There was a pretty good chance she would be starting school on Monday, meaning she had three days to not be completely clueless.

The shelf Dani had found held at least fifty books, one with a sapphire blue spine got her attention. She showed it to her bodyguard.

"The Dark Ages of Breckindale: Volume One, looks interesting."

Dani wouldn't have guessed a realm so colorful and bright would have been through a dark age. Maybe it wasn't as different from earth as she had believed.

"I can have it delivered to your room if you'd like," Anders offered, gesturing to one of the library guards.

"Sure," The more Dani could learn about Breckindale before Monday the better.

"And Anders," Dani said. "Thank you,"

This time her guard actually smiled. "My pleasure."

Chapter Nine

"So how was your first day in Breckindale?" Will flung his bag off of his shoulder and put it down at the edge of the grand staircase. "It would have been so much cooler if mom and dad didn't make me go to school today I'm sure."

"Probably," Dani said, mostly to appease her brother, "But it was actually pretty fun. Cornelius is really funny."

His eyes lit back up again. "Did he tell you about his pet dragon yet?" He grinned when she shook her head.

"I'll let him tell the story some other time, so all I'm going to say is that he got a dragon and had a wild time trying to tame it. But Cornelius let me name him Scorch so there's that."

"Dragons exist here?"

Will nodded enthusiastically. "Yep, and they're awesome. I tried to convince mom and dad to let me have one but they didn't want the palace to burn down."

"Probably best," Dani decided, nodding when her twin shook his head clearly offended. "I met the Magicals this morning."

Her brother glanced around quickly and then made a face. "How was Iris?" Clearly Dani wasn't the only twin who'd been rubbed the wrong way.

Dani shrugged. "I don't think she likes me very much," And that was putting it mildly.

"I still don't get why mom and dad keep her as an advisor if all she does is complain and argue but you aren't the problem. I'm pretty sure she's only nice to me because of what I can do to her when I'm king."

"What can you do to her when you're king?" Dani narrowed her eyes and nudged Will until he explained, picking up his bag and heading upstairs with her on his heels.

"Every monarch can either keep the previous council of Magicals or choose their own through votes and an election. Dad picked all new ones except for Cordelia and Milos who advised our grandfather his last two years."

Dani nodded, grinning. "And you don't plan on keeping Iris do you?"

Her brother's look was answer enough.

"She said something about my future today too," Though it was certainly more ominous than Will's. Her's involved a power that Dani needed to control and a future that was apparently chosen for her. None of it made any sense.

"What did she say this time?" Will asked, leading the way through the twisted upstairs hallways.

His frown only grew deeper after Dani had recounted the entire conversation and repeated the riddle a few times. The heir was just as stumped as the spare was when it came to the translation.

"I thought she was just talking about my royal role but Anders said I get to choose that myself."

"And he's right, you get to choose the role you want to play after graduation." But Will didn't. He'd been the future king since the moment he was born and it sounded like a pretty large burden for someone that young even if he was technically older than Dani by four minutes.

"She also mentioned how important it was that I learn to control my power," And Dani's skills in that department were sorely lacking.

Will screwed up his face. "Unfortunately Iris is right about that. Our powers are our strongest gift and our greatest weakness. If you can't control the power you were given then it's useless."

Dani wished her brother hadn't been quite so blunt. "I can shoot sparks out of my hands when I get upset, how am I supposed to control that?"

Will paused in the hall, thinking. "Keeping your emotions in check I guess. You said that you manifested after a boy made you mad right? Maybe you'll learn more about it during your training sessions."

When he started walking again Dani had to jog to keep up.

"Training?"

"At Crystalium we train with our powers twice a week."

"So everyone can learn how to use their powers correctly?"

"Yep,"

Dani let the information sink into her brain. "How did we get assigned our powers anyway?" And why couldn't she have gotten an easier one to handle!

"It depends," He shrugged but didn't stop walking. "Some powers are common in a certain family so they get passed down. Ours don't follow any pattern so our powers are chosen through our genetic coding."

Dani narrowed her eyes. "So it was completely random that I manifested as a sparker?" That couldn't be it. Nothing that important could have possibly been random.

Will shook his head madly. "No, our powers aren't randomly chosen for us. Sometimes the reasons aren't terribly obvious but you get a specific power for a reason."

So her power was given to her for a reason, a reason she didn't understand at all. Because the universe decided that she had to be a sparker and shouldn't read minds like her twin brother.

"So my genetic code decided I should be a sparker based on what?" Dani wasn't good at science without a formula to follow and unfortunately for her, magic followed nothing.

"Potential," Will let the word hang in the air between them. "And character."

That made even less sense! How could Dani's shy and quiet character have matched her with a power that was so unpredictable and dangerous?

"But I wasn't even born yet! How could my genes know what I was going to be like in the future?" The gears in Dani's head were spinning so fast she was starting to get dizzy.

"Magic," Will said, "I know it's hard to understand since you've only been around magic for a day but you'll start getting used to it soon."

Dani wasn't so sure about that, but she nodded anyway as they reached the hall where their bedrooms were.

"So are you excited for tomorrow?" Will asked, grinning again. Dani arched a brow. "What's tomorrow?"

Her brother's smile only grew. "Tomorrow mom and dad are hosting a reception."

Dani had to stop herself from gawking at him. Receptions were held for important people and dignitaries, definitely not an event for newly branded teenagers.

But it was the perfect place for a prince and princess.

"At Elthorne?" Dani was positive this was the first she was hearing of a reception, though evidently both her and Will were attending.

He nodded. "Both of our aunts are coming and I think our grandma is too. You'll get to meet them tomorrow before all of the guests arrive."

That was a loaded sentence if Dani had ever heard one and it took her a minute to mull it all over in her head. The thought of meeting more of her family was just as exciting and unnerving as completing her first duty as a princess.

"Do you go to these things a lot?"

Her twin nodded again. "Since I was seven pretty much but they'll be far less boring now that I have someone to hang out with."

Dani had never considered that her brother may have been lonely as an only child, especially since she herself had always been content with no siblings. But she figured knowing she had a twin but couldn't see him would have made things a lot harder.

"So what do we have to do at these events?"

Will tapped his chin. "Greet guests with our family and make small talk mostly. It's a lot more fun than it sounds." Of course he would say that if he'd been doing it for more than half of his life.

Playing host sounded fun. Talking to strangers made her nervous.

Dani frowned. "What will I say to them?"

"Just ask them if they are enjoying the reception, ask them about their families or the weather." This would have been a great time for Dani to share the fact that she had never made any friends on earth but she refrained, attempting to at least keep some of her dignity.

"What do I do if they ask me questions I'm not supposed to answer?" The idea of being sent into a room of strangers was just as appealing as having the horrifying scenario of the angry mob play in her nightmares every night for the next year.

"Try to steer the conversation away politely or just give them a standard but vague answer." Will was clearly a professional at small talk.

Dani nodded anyway, trying her best to memorize his tips and save them for the day after when she'd really need them. She had approximately twenty four hours until the reception, probably not enough time to completely transform into the perfect princess she was supposed to be.

But Dani was still going to spend every waking moment trying.

Chapter Ten

"How is this?" Dani emerged from her closet wearing a long sleeve navy gown Amandine had encouraged her to try on a few minutes prior.

"You look beautiful," Her mother promised, looking impossibly regal in a cranberry gown with diamonds along the bodice and edges of the skirt.

"This one it is then," Dani decided. "Now, what about my hair?"

"You like wearing your hair half up?" Amandine asked, her own hair in a braided bun on the nape of her neck.

Dani nodded. She had worn her hair half up the day she'd been moved to Breckindale and then again the day before.

"Well then why don't we just do that then?" Amandine gave a dazzling smile, walking over to help tie the front pieces of her hair back with a navy blue ribbon.

"How many people did you say were coming?" Dani tried not to squirm and mess up the tiny braids her mother was weaving out of the strands.

Her mother paused for a moment before answering. "The amount of guests doesn't matter,"

Once her hair was finished Dani spun to face her mother and narrowed her eyes.

Amandine relented. "The estimate I was given was in the two hundred range,"

Dani was going to faint before even making it downstairs.

Her mom clearly noticed, giving a reassuring smile that Dani didn't return. "Remember what we practiced yesterday?" After dinner the night before, Amandine had explained everything that she would need to do at the reception and walked her through it. She was prepared in theory anyway.

"Will I be standing next to Octavia or Beatrice?"

"Your aunt Octavia will be on your right and I will be on your left. Your grandmother will be between your father and I." Amandine explained.

Dani filed the information in her head. "And which one do I curtsy to?"
"Your grandmother because she is the former Queen consort." Her mother reminded gently.

"I may need lessons!" Dani resisted the urge to flop down on her bed, conceding to just sit at the edge of it instead.

"On what, darling?" Amandine prompted, her hands neatly folded in front of her.

"Being a princess," Dani grumbled, clutching a pillow to her chest. "Breckindale, everything above."

Amandine shook her head disapprovingly. "You are too hard on yourself," She promised. "Just give yourself some time to adjust."

Dani held the pillow tighter. "Everyone keeps saying that!"

"Because it's true," Her mother said. "When I attended my first reception your father and I had been married for only a month. I wasn't new to Breckindale nor the responsibilities of the royal family but I was still five times as panicked as you are."

"I'm pretty nervous," Dani held up her shimmery red hands as proof. As long as sparks didn't go flying at any point during the reception Dani would count it as a success.

Amandine smiled. "Perhaps, but you are handling it very well." Her compliment helped Dani's hands stop trembling slightly.

Dani gently set the pillow down beside her. "The reception is taking place in the music room?"

Much to her confusion, the music room held no musical instruments but her tour had proven that it was large enough to hold far more than two hundred people.

Her mother nodded. "But first we are greeting the guests in the oval hall," Dani had seen that the oval hall led into the side entrance of the music room when she'd gone exploring with Will the afternoon before.

Before Dani could ask any of the other questions swarming her brain, a guard she recognized as Amandine's bodyguard opened the door and stepped inside. "I apologize for the intrusion, your majesty but the king is requesting the presence of you and the princess downstairs immediately."

Amandine nodded. "Of course, thank you." Dani's mother followed her guard out into the hall and she reluctantly trailed behind.

"How are you doing?"

Anders met her there, walking beside her either to keep her company or to prevent her from fleeing.

Dani weighed her response. "A bit nervous but okay," Her hands had stopped their shaking and gone back to their normal color, all good signs.

Her bodyguard kept his expression passive. "That's to be expected for your first official appearance."

"What if I make a fool of myself?" Dani had cautiously been trying to ignore everything that she could do wrong but all the possibilities were hard to keep at bay.

"Simple," Anders said, "You won't." His faith in her was generous.

Dani frowned. "I see a face plant in my future," Combined with her nerves and the heels she was wearing, an impending disaster was a sure bet.

Anders gave a hint of a smile. "Such theatrics aren't common at these types of events."

Maybe Dani would make them a tradition.

She had been just about to voice that concern when a shriek pierced through her eardrums and echoed through the palace. Dani moved to the balcony to see what was going on.

"There's my delightful big brother!" The voice in question belonged to a woman with shoulder length dark hair wearing a yellow gown the same shade as the sun.

"That is your aunt Beatrice," Anders explained. "The Duchess of Clarence."

"Hello, Callan." A woman with slightly longer and straighter hair dipped a low curtsy and kissed Dani's father on his cheek. She wore an even stare like armor and had on a pale blue gown adorned with pearls.

"And that is your aunt Octavia," Anders relayed. "The Duchess of Bellenslow."

"Amandine!" Beatrice was the first to notice Dani's mother gliding down the staircase and the only one of the aunts who was positively beaming.

"Beatrice," Dani's mother beamed right back. "It's so good to see you." When the queen reached the foyer the two of them embraced.

From her high view point Dani could see her brother standing close to their father glancing around the foyer and up to the stairs. When he noticed her, he waved.

Dani carefully made her way down, holding onto the gold railing the entire time.

"There you are!" Callan gave a warm smile when they all spotted her, giving her a hand when she stepped off of the landing. Amandine moved to make room,keeping Dani in the middle of her parents.

"Octavia, Beatrice, this is Dani."

Before her father had even finished the introduction, Beatrice rushed to embrace her. "You are so grown up!" She released her,glancing at Callan instead. "She is so grown up!"

Aunt Beatrice switched glance to Octavia a split second later. "Isn't she gorgeous, Via?"

"She is very pretty," Octavia said,giving an approving nod and stepping back once more.

Dani wished she would be standing beside the fun aunt instead of the gloomy one.

Callan cleared his throat. "Where is mother? I was told she was arriving with the two of you."

"I did," A woman shorter than Will strode in, her floor length white gown flowing around her. Dani's grandmother had slight wrinkles around her face and streaks of gray in her dark bun.

"Mother, I am so glad you could join us." Callan took her hand and kissed her cheek.

"Well I wasn't about to miss the last reception of the season now was I." She embraced Amandine next, rolling her eyes playfully at her son.

Will stepped up next. "Hi grandma," He bowed first before kissing her cheek and embracing her. She swatted him with a smile.

The older woman shook her head, eyes dancing. "None of that, you're the future king here, not me!"

And then her eyes locked with Dani's and she let go of Will, gasping.

"When did Danielle return?" She stared back at Callan and Amandine, gown swishing at her feet.

Her grandmother hadn't needed to be reminded of Dani's name. She'd known it.

Amandine gave a patient smile. "Thursday night, Phillipa. She said, "Forgive us for not alerting you sooner."

"Forgiven." The older woman mumbled,moving closer to where Dani stood now slightly off to the side. The young princess dipped a curtsy. "And none from you either! Come give your grandmother a hug." And so Dani did.

And then she was released and her grandmother crossed her arms and stared at the family assembled before her. "Well what are you all still doing in the foyer? Guests will be arriving any minute now. Let's move!"

And with a final glance at each other, they all did.

Chapter Eleven

Amandine's estimate of just over two hundred guests turned out to be a huge understatement and after shaking the first two hundred and fifty guest's hands Dani's own was exhausted. She would have asked her mother how many more brytlyns were on their way but she felt that would come across as rude so she refrained.

"You look to be enjoying yourself," Octavia gave a thin smile, the first Dani had received since they'd met. Once the princess realized her aunt was truly talking to her she prepared a response.

"I like meeting everyone," Dani said truthfully. If being a princess meant being acknowledged and not overlooked all the time maybe her role wasn't all that bad.

Octavia nodded, offering another smile, this one amused. "How's your hand?" She said it knowingly and Dani remembered who she was talking to. Octavia had been in the same royal position Dani was, the younger sister of the future king and the daughter of the current one, she must have shook

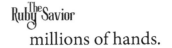

millions of hands.

The princess shook her right hand out beside her. "About to fall off." When Octavia let out the briefest of laughs Dani was glad she had made the joke.

"You get used to it," Octavia advised. "Give it a year and you'll have a hand of steel." This time Dani couldn't tell if her aunt was kidding or not. Her tone was just as stoic as Dani's bodyguard's was.

"That would help the throbbing." Dani agreed, preparing her hand again as a handful of more brytlyns in finery entered the hall. It was a great relief when only twenty more brytlyns arrived,completing the guest list and giving everyone's hands some peace when they moved on to mingling.

As much as small talk made Dani's stomach feel like a butterfly sanctuary it involved less handshakes and for that she was immeasurably grateful.

"You're doing well," Anders said, looking proud and mildly impressed when he escorted her to meet more of the guests. Each royal had a certain section that they would linger in to make small talk before switching to another once they'd met everyone.

"Thanks," Dani said, allowing herself a smile. She'd been doing well so far. "I'm a lot less shy here than I was on earth, Anders. Isn't that odd?"

Her guard shook his head. "No, perhaps that is simply because here you have a better outlet to develop your social skills,"

"Maybe," Dani agreed,pausing when they reached a blond haired woman in a violet gown.

"Your royal highness, may I introduce the Duchess of Orvirr." Anders had been in charge of her introductions the entire reception.

"It's nice to meet you," Dani extended her hand like she had before. This time she used her left.

"The pleasure is mine,your highness." The duchess said,giving a dazzling smile as she shook her hand. "Welcome back to Breckindale."

Dani smiled politely in return. "Thank you, I'm very glad to be home."

"Your mother told me earlier that you will start at Crystalium soon?" The duchess continued,giving Dani an excuse to not bring up the weather once more.

"My first day is Monday," Dani replied. "I'm very much looking forward to it." That may have been stretching the truth slightly but since she'd been told the good news during breakfast, Dani really had gotten interested to see what a brytlyn school was like.

The duchess's smile only grew. "My son is in your grade level.

Perhaps the two of you will be in the same group."

"Yes," Dani agreed, "It would be nice to have him in my group." She had hoped her and Will would be in the same pod at Crystalium, but apparently some of his best friends were twins and they had all been split up.

"I apologize, your grace, but the princess's "presence has been requested." Anders stepped in, and after a quick goodbye Dani was being led through the crowd of people. "There is someone who wants to have a word with you," he explained, gesturing to a shorter woman in a red gown who was waiting expectantly.

"Princess Danielle, this is Amana, the Countess of Penketh." Anders made the introductions once again and then stepped a short distance away.

"It is lovely to finally make your acquaintance, your highness." The countess said brightly. "Having such an intense power like your sparks can be such a burden so I just wanted to offer my support now that you've manifested."

Dani plastered a smile on her face to hide her shock. "That's very kind of you,"

Her parents had said that they wanted no one but the family, their advisors, and Elthorne's staff to know what her power was. If it hadn't been released to the public then how could a countess already know about it?

Chapter Twelve

"Maybe the Magicals told the public that you were a sparker after all," Will suggested, though he sounded far more hopeful than sure.

Dani paced the length of her bedroom twice before answering. "I don't know!"

Will sighed. "I really don't think the Magicals would have disobeyed the orders mom and dad gave them."

Dani hoped so. Especially if the order insured that their young princess wouldn't become a spectacle before she knew how to handle the attention.

"How could Amana have known about it?"

The reception had only ended an hour before and while her parents were speaking with her aunts and grandmother Dani had been filling her brother in on everything she'd been told. Now it was Will's turn to be frustrated. "I don't know!"

Dani was as confused as her twin brother. And Amana's words

of support had been just as vague as Iris's riddle the day before.

"What about Octavia and Beatrice, how much do they know?" Will suggested, arms crossed over his chest.

Dani shrugged. "I assume not very much they didn't even know I came back,"

Will nodded. "And grandma didn't have a clue either, besides, they wouldn't have told any nobles that sort of personal stuff about us no matter how critical it was."

"So our family is out," Dani didn't feel as relieved as she should have. "Are you sure the Magicals wouldn't have told anyone if mom and dad said not to?"

"Yes."

"Well then does Iris despise me enough to spill?"

"If she values her job she wouldn't say a word. Discretion is mandatory for everyone close to the four of us."

Dani shook her head, her conversation with the Magicals running through her brain like a movie.

"Iris likes being a Magical way too much," They'd only met once but it was evident just how much Iris enjoyed the perks her position gave her.

"So who does that leave," Will didn't phrase it as a question so

Dani didn't give him an answer. Not because she was being difficult but because she didn't have one for him.

No one. It left absolutely no one. She was back to the beginning.

"You could ask Giselle just to be sure Iris didn't leak anything; she wouldn't lie."

"I tried after I finished talking to Amana but I couldn't fight my way through the mob." Dani had tried to get Giselle's attention from across the room but she had failed miserably.

Will didn't look surprised. "It's hard at these kinds of events. Maybe try scheduling a conference with her?"

"I can do that?"

Her brother nodded. "The Magicals work for dad and mom but their jobs are technically to assist all members of the royal family. If you need to talk to Giselle you can."

"How much time do I have before we're leaving?" It was already well into the afternoon and the Callisto family had invited them for dinner at Umbergrove.

"Not enough to arrange a meeting, Dani."

"Tomorrow then." Dani nodded resolutely.

Will nodded, his serious expression changing instantly to a mischievous grin. "But we do have enough time to go check

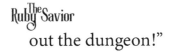

out the dungeon!"

Dani's jaw nearly dropped. "Elthorne has a dungeon?"

"Yes, Dani. Elthorne has a dungeon and it happens to be very dark and creepy and littered with cool relics."

"Creepy and dark really isn't my thing." Dani gave an apologetic smile.

"Come on, we can reclaim some twin bonding time we missed out on for thirteen years." Will gave a fake pout that only earned an inquisitive glance from his sister.

"Can't we have twin bonding time while not touring a dungeon?"

Will sighed. "I guess but it won't be as entertaining. Oh and I absolutely refuse to go with you to the library so you can pick up more books!" He pointed to the hefty stack already piled high on her desk.

Dani grinned. "I was just going to head to the library to get more actually,"

"I won't stop you from the torture that is books then, have fun," Her brother lamented.

"Where are you going?"

Will sighed loudly. "To do my cipher homework. I will see you later."

"Good luck with that then." Dani murmured, letting her brother head into his bedroom before meeting her bodyguard in the hall.

She had told Will she planned to go get more books from a library and she was. Just probably not from the one he was expecting.

Anders didn't look surprised when she headed in the direction of the grand staircase.

"Downstairs library?" He asked.

"Downstairs library," She repeated.

"Your brother was right about your selection," Her bodyguard mused. "The desk may crack under the weight if you add more books to it."

Dani paused on the fifth step to the bottom,turning around. "You can never have too many books,Anders." She said solemnly, taking the final few steps two at a time and then leading the way to the downstairs library.

"I suppose," he called, following closely behind as Dani rushed through the long corridor that led to the small library at the end. She was looking for one specific book. One with a violet cover and a very interesting portrait inside.
She remembered exactly where she'd left it the day prior,right

where it still was supposed to be when she entered.

Unfortunately, when she got there her book wasn't.

"Maybe the staff moved it when they cleaned earlier today?" Anders suggested, already scanning the shelves calmly for the exact book Dani was looking for.

"I don't see it in here," Dani replied, frowning in thought.

Nor did she see it anytime in the next five minutes. She kept looking under the sofa, in the corners, on the shelves, but no hiding spot concealed her book.

It had vanished out of thin air.

Chapter Thirteen

The third strange occurrence since her move. That was how Dani chose to think of her missing book which paired with Amana's support and Iris's riddle was adding something of a mystery to her new life in Breckindale.

Will hadn't been concerned in the slightest when she had rushed upstairs to tell him about what had happened in the downstairs library. Still, Dani couldn't shake the feeling that something was off here. She hadn't even been in Breckindale for a complete three days and weird things were already happening to her.

What those things had to do with her was another question. Three days before, Dani had been a normal teenager who only worried about kids saying mean things to her and now she had a magic power that was making her life infinitely more complicated.

The power she hadn't used in three days because she was terrified of it.

"Would you like me to ask Grantham if he has seen it?" Anders watched near the door while Dani thumbed through another book she had found.

"That's okay I can ask him later," Dani felt horrible about her dramatics already and inconveniencing their butler wouldn't make things much better. And as Will had reminded her, losing a book in a huge castle was more unfortunate than suspicious.

Instead, Dani continued skimming through what appeared to be a very detailed log of the powers Stallard family members had manifested through the generations. True to her brother's word, their family didn't share a certain handful of powers that were passed down; they had dozens.

Shadows and Speeds and Flames and Freezers and Sensors and Lighters and Winders and Transferers and Teleporters just to name a few.

The last entry in the book had been Callan, who Dani now knew was a Teleporter. She thought it a bit odd that her aunts and brother hadn't been included in the log but the book had been tucked securely in between two larger ones on the middle shelf so maybe it had just been forgotten.

"Are you coming to Umbergrove with us?" Dani looked up, closing her book.

Anders nodded. "Of course, you need protection wherever you go." His warning about danger and threats loomed back to the forefront of her mind.

"Thank you," Dani ignored the way her hands resumed to shake and warm with a shimmering red coating. It was ridiculous to be so nervous about meeting one family when she'd already met so many people earlier but the memo wasn't reaching her emotions that were currently threatening to rain sparks down on the palace.

"Everett and Eldridge are nice boys,Dani. There is no need to be worried." Anders may not have been able to read her thoughts but he sure was good at noticing things.

Dani wasn't used to having friends. The idea shouldn't have been quite as troubling as it seemed to be,blossoming worry into her head like a flower bearing fresh petals.

"I didn't have any friends on earth,Anders." The closest she had ever come was being assigned a small group for projects in elementary school.

"Well you will make two tonight and many more at Crystalium." Her guard promised, sounding twenty times as confident as Dani felt.

"I would like that,"

He nodded. "And you'll have more brytlyns then just your brother to keep you company during events."

"Oh yeah, mom did say they were noble."

"Quite a few of your classmates will be."
Dani still had more than a day before she'd start school but

the jitters were already well rooted. She didn't know what to expect in a brytlyn school and that alone was enough to make her shiver.

"How will I know where to go on the first day?" Dani had considered her old school to be decently large but from Will's description of Crystalium her middle school had been a shoebox.

"I'm sure the boys will help with that as will your brother and I." He reassured her. "I can personally promise that you will not get lost." And Dani believed him.

"Do you think I'll like my new school?" She certainly hoped so. Now that she wasn't invisible the idea of going back to that was an unsettling proposition though one that was close to impossible.

"I do," Anders said, perfectly assured.

At least at this school Dani had a chance. Her name and title all but confirmed it.
Crystalium would be the official end of the invisible girl.

"Where do the Callistos live anyway?" There were no homes close to Elthorne as far as Dani could see yet no nobles had complained about their transportation. Unless blinking had been used they couldn't have lived very far.

"Their home is about twenty minutes away by coach," Anders answered. "Blinking is unnecessary for such a short trip."

"Are there neighborhoods in Breckindale?" Maybe the nobility all lived together in scattered cul de sacs not too far from Elthorne.

For the first time since Dani had met him, Anders seemed stumped by a question. "What is a neighborhood?"

And that was answer enough.

Chapter Fourteen

"The Callistos live here?" Dani's eyes nearly popped out of their sockets staring out the coach window at the sprawling mansion in front of them.

Anders had said that the Callisto family had a home so Dani had imagined a modest house like the one she had lived in on earth. This was only slightly smaller than Elthorne Palace.

Will grinned and waved at the family outside. "Welcome to Umbergrove,"

"Does everyone have big houses here?" Dani had assumed theirs was only larger because it was a royal castle but Umbergrove was massive. Like really massive.

"Only nobles mostly but Breckindale is a large realm," Will explained. "The amount of people living in it would only be slightly smaller than the amount living on earth.

Dani had to keep her jaw from dropping.

"Do they have bodyguards too?" They looked important

enough to warrant them for sure.

Will gave a smile. "Nope. That's just us,"

Amandine's bodyguard who'd been seated at the front of the coach opened her door but Dani waited for Anders before she climbed out and followed her family up to the entrance.

A man with tanned skin and wavy hair went right up to Callan while a woman with bright caramel colored hair embraced Amandine, leaving an older girl and two boys, all with varying shades of auburn hair.

"Dani, this is Bree, Everett, and Eldridge." Will had moved over to where Dani stood, pointing to each one in turn.

"Hey," Bree said, her voice light and kind.

She had bright green eyes and long hair curled at the ends. She was taller than her brothers but not by much even with their four year age gap.

Everett and Eldridge were paternal twins with the same amber eyes and wavy hair that looked more brunette than red. The latter was a smidge taller than the former and had wavier hair. Everett grinned. Eldridge nodded.

"Nice to meet you," Dani's nerves melted away when she returned the smiles. They all seemed nice. She'd be fine.

Everett turned to watch the adults for a moment and then

let out a sigh. "Bree, can we go in now?" They'll be out here forever." The last part was directed at Dani and was said in stage whisper.

Bree shrugged. "Sure, we aren't needed anymore." She opened the double doors and led the way into the foyer where two grand staircases awaited, both leading up to the second floor. Bree went up the one on the far right, while the boys led Dani up the opposite one.

"They won't even notice we're inside," Eldridge agreed quietly, shooting a knowing glance at the doors.

Will nodded from beside Everett. "This happens every time."

"They start reminiscing about their school days and then it's all over!" Everett complained,though Dani could tell he was suppressing a smile.

"How long have they been friends for?" She knew Crystalium lasted for eight years but Will hadn't told what year the Callistos and their parents had become friends.

"Their second year like us," Everett answered,staring straight at Dani. "That's probably why they've been so anxious for us to finally meet you." He and Will made it to the landing a step before Dani and Eldridge did, giving them a minute to get caught up before launching back into polite questioning. "Have your parents been talking about it as much as ours have?"

Dani shook her head. "They mentioned it earlier today when we heard about the invitation but that was it." Her parents had been far too busy helping her adjust to the realm they also had to rule.

Everett narrowed his eyes and crossed his arms, considering her answer. "How different is earth from here?" The four of them were walking in a line now and Dani was between both Callisto boys with Will beside Everett on the other side.

"Well where I lived there was no king or queen that ruled us. Instead of coaches and blinking we traveled by cars and planes and buses. Schools were smaller and there were different ones for certain grade levels. Oh, and there is no magic there." The last fact seemed pretty obvious but it felt wrong not to list it.

"How do they prolong their lifespans without magic?" Eldridge asked, clearly just as confused as his brother and Dani's were.

"They don't." Dani answered simply, realizing for the first time what that meant. Her old classmates would be wrinkled and elderly by the time Dani would only look like an adult. Her human parents would be gone.

She shook the thoughts away, turning to glance at Eldridge. "You're a lighter right?" After reading about the different powers earlier Dani was very interested to get to see a few in person, especially one that seemed so cool.

He beamed and nodded. "We only turned thirteen a month ago so I haven't really gotten the hang of my light yet," He snapped his fingers and a small orb of bright light formed,illuminating everything.

"That's incredible!" Dani gasped when he twisted his hand and the light shaped into a star.

"Thanks," Eldridge swiped his hand through the star,disintegrating it. If this was his power after only a month Dani couldn't wait to see how good it got with more practice.

She switched her gaze to Everett. "What can you do?" Dani knew that he was a sensor but no one had explained what it meant. Will hadn't offered any clarification but a tight lipped smile. It would have been helpful if the power log wrote what each talent meant but then again it would be redundant for everyone but her.

"I can read emotions,"

"How?" She hoped the process wasn't as creepy as what transferers could do. Knowing her thoughts weren't always private was incredibly unnerving.

"Every emotion gives off a certain colored aura that only sensors can see. Right now yours is green so you must be curious." Everett's explanation made perfect sense and left her with a million other questions. He wasn't wrong.

Eldridge nudged her shoulder. "You're a sparker right? Our parents mentioned it earlier but I don't think I've ever heard of that power before."

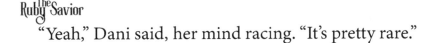

"Yeah," Dani said, her mind racing. "It's pretty rare."

Favian and Genevieve had been the ones who told the boys what her power was. They hadn't been told by the Magicals through an announcement. They were in the nobility.

If Everett was reading her emotions at that moment he would have seen the color for relief and an even stronger aura of dread.

If the Magicals truly hadn't announced her power and it hadn't been leaked through the nobility then there was no explanation Dani could come up with as to how Amana had figured it out.

Chapter Fifteen

"Okay, this is amazing." Dani stared up at the high domed ceiling covered in glistening stars of all colors of the spectrum.

Eldridge and Everett had given her a tour of Umbergrove which was now concluding in the planetarium. Dani was grateful for any distraction from the puzzle pieces trying to fit together in her head and this one was the best one she could've ever imagined.

"Bree used to be afraid of the dark so our parents turned this room into a planetarium for all of us." Everett explained, his face bathed in purple light.

"It really is incredible," Dani had been afraid of the dark when she was younger too but the solution to that problem had been a ladybug nightlight.

She nudged her twin brother. "I wish we had something like this at Elthorne."

Will grinned mischievously. "If we pretend that you're a

scaredy cat then we could."

"Mom and dad would never believe that, we'd have to say that it's you." Dani smiled innocently back, earning a laugh from both Callisto boys.

"It's a huge help for studying for our stars and constellations class," Everett said. "That's what we use it for now anyway."

Dani watched a yellow star soar overhead. "Is that a fun class?" She'd never learned much about the solar system at any of her old schools but these stars piqued her interest.

Everett nodded. "We study star maps and different types of constellations that are seen from Breckindale. It's one of my favorites."

Dani hadn't realized that earth and Breckindale had different stars but she probably should have. Different realms meant different solar systems; it meant something entirely new.

"Stars are colorful here," She let that incredible thought sink in as a red beam of light spun in circles high above her head.

"What do the ones near earth look like?" Eldridge wondered, his question earning Everett and Will's attention as well. Two pairs of identical eyes and a pair identical to hers staring straight at her.

Dani wasn't quite sure how to explain them.
"They just look like tiny white specks of light," She said lamely.

She couldn't come up with anything better.

"Do they have magical properties?" Everett asked. It took Dani a moment to conclude that Breckindale's did.

She shook her head. "Nope, they are just normal." It was hard to explain what normal meant when everything in her new life including the people were extraordinary.

Everett only waited a second before speaking again. "Have you received your schedule yet for Crystalium?"

Will had explained to them during the tour that Dani would be starting school on Monday and both boys had spent the time since answering her many questions.

"I don't think so," Dani said, shooting an uncertain glance at her brother. "But I have a meeting with Sir Lechin Monday morning so maybe I'll get it then." She'd been informed that Sir Lechin was the school's advisor when being shown the formal sitting room.

Eldridge nodded. "Your group assignment will be on it so I guess you'll find out if you're in one of ours then."

"I hope I am, I only know one other person who goes and from what I've heard me and Will won't be in the same group anyway." Technically Dani also knew that the son of the Duchess of Orvirr was in her grade too but since she didn't even know his name she didn't really count him.

"Me too," Everett agreed, "But even if you are put in another group we all will have the same lunch time and physical education session."

"Everyone at Crystalium is nice though," Eldridge added. "I'm sure you'll make friends in whatever group you are in."

The princess smiled. If an actual student said she'd be fine then maybe Dani really did have a chance.

Bree stuck her head in before Dani could respond. "Dinner is ready!" She announced,giving a bright smile and then walking back out to the hall.

Everett and Will led the way out, waiting until their respective twins had followed before following Bree back around the upstairs of the manor and down the right staircase.

The dining room in Umbergrove was colored in all neutral tones containing a long brass table with ornate chairs, a glass stained window, and a portrait of the family that hung on the wall. It must have been a few years old since the boys were much smaller and Bree had bangs.

While Everett chatted animatedly to Callan and Will talked to Genevieve and Favian, Dani turned to Eldridge on her right. "Do you like your power?" She asked quietly. The closest power she had found to her own was Eldridge's, but unlike her he didn't seem to fear what he could create.

"I'm glad I have my power instead of the power Everett and dad share," His lips turned up into an uneasy smile, it looked pained. "But sometimes controlling the light is difficult. That's what I've been working on the most with my instructor during training sessions."

Dani nodded, relief washing over her. "I haven't used my power since I manifested last Thursday," It felt good admitting her fear to someone who actually understood. "My sparks reflect my emotions and until I learn control I don't want to use it."

"Maybe when you start training with your power you'll feel more comfortable using it. That's what helped me," Eldridge suggested finally.

"Maybe,"

Eldridge managed another smile. "I guess the outgoing powers are given to the introverted brytlyns now, it's great."

Dani gave a wiry smile in return. "So great,"

Everett spun around to face them, eyes narrowed. "Why do you two look so serious? Dinner is supposed to be a fun event." He tossed a purple vegetable up in the air and caught it in his mouth with a grand flourish. Will clapped at the brilliant display.

"I don't think that's how you're supposed to eat that." Dani held up her fork and waved it like a magic wand near Everett.

Will shook his head, joining in and preparing to throw one of his own vegetables. "His way is better,"

When Dani turned to Eldridge her friend was shaking his head grimly, though he wasn't hiding his laugh very well with a cough.

"I bet by this time next week you'll be so good at using your power there'll be no need for worrying anymore." Eldridge promised, watching his twin attempt to balance a fork on his nose.

Dani turned just in time to see her brother try the same thing. "I really hope so,"

Dinner ended and Dani and her family left some time after that, leaving for home feeling much better than she had when she had left. She had friends now and the worry in her stomach fueled by Crystalium had fizzled out into nothing. Eldridge's advice had helped the most, giving her hope for controlling her power even as she arrived at Elthorne an hour later.

"You were right," Dani told Anders as she made her way up to her bedroom. Her bodyguard was on a winning streak.

"I'm glad you made friends," He said, a hint of a smile appearing. "Not that I ever doubted it."

"I should listen to you more often." Dani agreed, her eyebrows raising when he let out what sounded like a snort.

"That would be beneficial, Dani." To Anders credit he only

gloated a bit.

"Is that what the instructors at school will call me? I haven't gone by Danielle since I was five years old."

Her bodyguard shook his head. "One of the main principles of Crystalium Academy is equality so yes depending on your instructors preference you will either be addressed by your first name or called Miss Stallard."

Dani nodded, she'd been so used to her last name being Cayden all her life hearing Stallard was bittersweet. But the last name thing was standard across all realms it seemed and for reasons even she didn't understand it did help the dull ache in her heart.

"Do I have anything planned tomorrow, Anders?" Dani forced herself to focus on her first priority: meeting with Giselle.

"I do not believe so," Anders answered, taking the last turn into her hallway. "But I was told that your school supplies arrived earlier today. They are in your father's office in case you want to pack your bag."

Dani nodded, adding it to her mental to do list as she reached her bedroom door. "Thanks Anders, goodnight."

"Goodnight, Dani." Anders took his usual position outside her door, closing it behind him and leaving her room basking in the moonlight seeping in through the wall of windows.
Dani grabbed the top book off of her pile on the desk and

raced to her bed, nearly coming crashing down when her toes collided with something thick and heavy on the floor.

"What the... " The last word was lodged in her throat as her eyes stared down at the violet covered volume below her.

The missing book hadn't been on her floor before that and she had checked twice. If her eyelids didn't feel quite so heavy Dani might've found that interesting but instead she just picked up both books and snuggled into her bed.

The missing book seemed much more interesting than the one from the pile about Breckindale's geography so she picked that one to read. It started off with a long introduction of the Stallard line and only started getting interesting when she reached chapter five entitled *The Great War* and excitedly, Dani pulled the book closer to get a good look.

As the royal family primed for the annual peace summit held every spring at Arnbridge Castle, a group of rebels had something much darker in store. The Order of the Raven as the organization came to be known attacked the castle and its residents emerging the realm into chaos as citizens and nobles alike turned against each other in a frenzied attempt to find the culprits and restore peace.

The Stallard family was forced into exile only a month later following further breaches of security at the castle and threats against the young heir Crown Prince Bren. On the first anniversary of the takeover Princess Delacour came of age and manifested her power while in exile. Against the wishes of her family she escaped from their safe house and bravely chose to fight back against the organization who had taken over her realm.

It was autumn of that year when Delacour challenged the leader of the organization: Hereen who was a powerful and well trained winder to a battle for the throne and using her power was able to defeat her.

Delacour's power was the first of its kind and the princess announced that she had been referring to herself as a Sparker due to the ruby red sparks she was able to shoot out of her hands. The princess was named the Savior of Breckindale, a title that would continue to be well respected as Breckindale resumed on into a time of peace.

The title was claimed to have been prophesied by the well known clairvoyant Gernon Cryt who also foresaw the princess dying in combat at the young age of eighteen to which his vision was morbidly correct. Before her tragic death, the clairvoyant warned her that the title of Savior would be given once again to the next Sparker in the Stallard line, destined to save the realm just as bravely as her ancestor and whose life would end tragically in combat at the same ripe age of eighteen.

Dani slammed the book shut, shoving it to the edge of her bed and letting it fall to the floor with a satisfying and starting thump.

She was a descendant of Delacour, the only sparker in the entire realm with the qualifications written in a deep black ink.

It had to be her.

Dani gave herself a moment, tears pooling in her eyes and her breath ragged as if she had run a mile. Her hands shook with more force than ever, a slick coating of shimmering red forming a layer around them.

She forced herself off of her bed and stood there for a moment more in shock, forcing herself to pick the book back up.

Then she ran to get her parents.

Chapter Sixteen

The Magicals arrived by the time Dani was situated on one of the sofas, frozen in a ball.

As soon as she had shown the pages to her mom and dad the palace had been a flurry of activity. The high advisors had been summoned, extra guards stationed, and the book had been taken away. No one had given her an explanation for what she had read or why.

Dani had wanted to keep the book, hoping that the more she scoured the page the easier the truth would be to understand but she hadn't been given much of a choice. She didn't even know where her book even was.

"They're here!" A guard Dani didn't recognize called as faint silhouettes appeared in the hall. Giselle rushed in first, kneeling down in front of Dani, her baby blue cloak swishing dramatically behind her.

"Are you okay?" Her eyes flooded in concern, waiting for Dani to say something.

Dani didn't know how to answer. Since reading the book a steady stream of sparks had flooded from her hands and around the palace in swirling waves.

She couldn't stop or control them. They weren't after anyone in particular and left the brytlyns who encountered them alone. Dani wondered if this was because she wasn't mad at any certain person, not this time. This time she was confused and scared.

For better or worse the sparks were conveying the tangled emotions perfectly.

So Dani chose the truth. "Not really," Giselle was fully capable of reading her thoughts anyway so there was no reason for her to lie.

"Giselle we have the book," Grennet strode in next, concerned, he crouched beside Giselle when he saw the small princess curled up. "How are you doing?"

Dani gave a half hearted sigh. "Good news, I'm not scared of using my power anymore." She let another flurry of ruby red light float above her left hand. They weren't evil like she had thought earlier. She made a mental note to tell Eldridge that he had been right.

Grennet gave a weary grin. "Focusing on the positives, good." He stood, giving Giselle a hand up. "We'll be right back." They left her to her misery, walking out to join the shadowed silhouettes in the hall which Dani assumed were the Magicals conferring, most likely with her parents.

Will had been with her until only a few minutes earlier when Amandine had called him over. Dani had been too numb to argue. She'd been too numb to do anything.

She wasn't lonely for long though and Anders walked in only a few moments after Giselle and Grennet left.

Dani picked her head up from resting on her knees to look at him. "Is the prophecy coming true already? Are we under attack?" The passage from the book was still fresh in her mind, keeping her nerves on edge.

Anders set his jaw tight. "No, unfortunately there was a security breach not too long ago." His weapon was still sheathed and he looked calm so Dani let herself breath.

"So we aren't under attack?" The soldiers stationed in the foyer and in every hall had given the opposite impression. Dani had descended the second floor to see them all in formation with swords at the ready and panicked.

Her bodyguard shook his head. "If it helps, this has nothing to do with an attack of any kind."

His promise helped a little. Or at least it did until the entirety of the Magical Council entered, faces grim and shadows under their eyes. Dani's family entered right behind, guards in tow and looking like they'd seen ghosts. Will moved to sit beside her while their parents sat on either side.

The Magicals formed the same line they had the day before and just like last time Dani glanced first at Grennet and Giselle hoping to see even the slightest bit of reassurance in their expressions. Anything to make her feel better about any of her new discoveries.

"Congratulations Dani, you are the Savior of Breckindale." Ronan didn't smile nor did he seem to mean the congratulations. Dani did not blame him.

"Thank you," Dani felt wrong saying the words. Being savior didn't feel like an accomplishment worth any praise; it felt like a job she hadn't signed up for and didn't want. A death sentence.

Her lips formed a narrow line. "What happens now?" Dani's racing brain was utterly blank, just as exhausted and frozen as the rest of her.

Ronan raised a bushy eyebrow. "For you, nothing. We will launch an investigation as soon as we can." How could nothing change when she was prophesied to die in five years?

"What about the security breach?" Anders wouldn't lie about something so serious not at a time like this.

Iris flipped her hair over her shoulder. "There was," She didn't look anywhere near as concerned as the words seemed to demand, instead seeming more annoyed at the situation than anything else.

"Well then why aren't you panicking?" Dani needed answers more than any of the sympathy she could tell everyone else wanted to give. As much as she was grateful for it, nothing could change what just happened to her.

Arabella gave a patient hint of a smile. "The breach was not as serious as I'm sure you're fearing."

"It really wasn't much of a breach at all." Grennet jumped in, his words chosen carefully. He knew something else and wasn't telling.

Dani frowned. "Now I'm confused," The Magicals were just beating around the bush now and she was sick of it.

"The last few paragraphs that describe the prophecy were not there previously." Giselle finally broke the horrible silence. "And because of that fact there is reason to believe that an intruder entered Elthorne and wrote it in before delivering it back to your bedroom."

"An intruder," Dani mumbled, "In Elthorne?" Wasn't the palace supposed to be the most secure place in the entirety of Breckindale?

"That is why it is being called a security breach." Iris pursed her lips and smiled, standing out amongst the gloomy bunch beside her.

Dani was ignoring the tempting urge to roll her eyes.

"I understand that. I'm just confused on how you knew the note had been added. I found it in the smaller library downstairs tucked into a shelf and covered in dust." Dani said through gritted teeth.

Iris didn't seem the type to care much about books or reading. She wouldn't have done a thorough search of a library at any time, especially if the library was filled with family journals and power logs.

"Because we found this outside Elthorne when we arrived." Dani's least favorite advisor was using her sugary sweet tone again, treating her like a wide eyed toddler who needed everything watered down. If she had more energy Dani would have sent some of her sparks towards the woman and laughed as she flailed. Unfortunately that would be very rude and this was not the time to laugh.

Especially when Dani was handed a golden medallion in the shape of a soaring eagle. Carved into the wing was her name. Carved below it was the word *savior*.

Chapter Seventeen

"They know who I am." Dani laid the medallion in her shaking hand and traced the engraving with her thumb.

Whoever had sent the gift clearly knew who she was and where she lived. More importantly they knew what role she'd be forced to play in the future.

That sent a chill down Dani's spine and a fresh flurry of sparks out of her hands. She only barely managed to calm herself before even more shot out and hit her twin brother in the face.

"Yes," Grennet uttered, his jaw tight and glance frustrated. When Dani turned to look at the Magicals and then her family they all wore a similar expression. Anger. Confusion. Guilt.

Dani curled herself into a tighter ball, tucking her chin into her knees and wrapping her shimmer coated hands around herself. It took a moment before she could force her mouth to produce words.

"What does this mean?"

"That the author of your note has ways of gathering information," Edon muttered. "Information only those in this room are aware of."

"Could they have teleported?" Will asked, eyebrows furrowed in concentration. "Dani told me earlier that her book was missing and then it conveniently appeared in her room? It doesn't make sense!"

It didn't make sense to Dani either; she just didn't have the heart to admit it.

"It's possible," Cordelia considered softly, "It would explain how they managed to get past the security. If they teleported right into Dani's bedroom they would bypass all of the guards stationed."

Dani nodded her agreement.

"And Anders was with me this evening at Umbergrove so there were no guards in my hall."

"If they can teleport in, how do we prevent them from continuing to leave messages?" Amandine didn't sound like a mother anymore. This time she really did sound like a queen demanding her subjects.

"Do you think whoever is behind this is going to contact me again?" Dani asked, turning to her mother.

Amandine didn't reply, but from the way she and the Magicals were looking at her Dani could tell that the answer was yes.

"Guards," Callan decided, voice firm. "She'll need a full security team with her at all times." He glanced up at Anders. "You'll lead it?"

Dani's bodyguard gave a curt nod.

"What about school?" Will asked, turning to face their father. "Can Dani still go?"

Dani unfurled herself out of her ball enough to peer at her father. As much as the prophecy frightened her, staying locked up in Elthorne with guards at all times sounded downright boring. Saviors didn't hide away; they fought.

"I suppose with a sizable amount of armed guards you can go." Callan did not look thrilled with his decision.

Anders clearly did not see the way Dani shook her head over and over when he nodded. "I can go to the academy in the morning. I've seen some of the newest graduates and they are quite impressive."

He also must've not noticed the glare Dani gave him following his suggestions.

"Brilliant," At least her father seemed thrilled by the idea as did her mother,though she looked more relieved.

"Prophecies can't be prevented." Dani mumbled, another

stream of sparks flowing out of her hands. With or without guards she was doomed.

"This will be the first," Her father replied, his confidence unwavering. "You will have a team as soon as possible and that is final."

"But what about until then?" Amandine spoke up. "Tonight at the very least we'll need something else to protect her."

Dani shook her head. "I'll be fine tonight, mom. If they wanted to give me another message tonight that already would have."

Giselle nodded. "Dani is correct, if they had another message for her it would have come with the note and the medallion."

"I suppose," Her father conceded, sharing a look with her mother.

"By the time we will start our investigation you'll be heavily protected." Giselle promised, though Dani could tell the last part was for Callan and Amandine's sole benefit.

I'll be back with an update as soon as I can.

Dani nodded, resisting the urge to jump back when the message came through.

I have questions.

She repeated the words over and over until Giselle gave half a nod.

I know.

Giselle's tone in the message was weary. Everyone in the room looked weary.

"I'll set up a conference as soon as we learn something." This time Giselle said the words out loud.

"Thank you," Dani said, and then the Magicals filed back out to the hallway and her parents followed. Will didn't move from his spot beside her.

"You should go to bed." Her brother said, his dark circles surely rivaling Dani's own.

"So should you." Dani replied, stifling her yawn. Sleep was far too tempting and all too impossible now.

Will gave a sad smile. "I'll try if you will,"

"Deal," Dani shook his hand resolutely and forced both of them up off the sofa. For the first time in nearly an hour sparks weren't flying around her and no knots filled her stomach.

"How are guards supposed to help my situation?" Dani asked Anders as he followed her to the grand staircase. "If you guys intervene in whatever battle I lose, it won't end any better."

"The idea is that you will never have to fight in that battle,

Dani." Anders replied calmly, his face a mask of steel.

"I don't think I really have a choice." Admitting it made everything feel truly and completely real and Dani didn't know what to do.

She was going to die at eighteen years old.

She would save the realm but not herself.

For the slightest of moments Anders wore a concerned expression that matched the ones everyone else had worn just moments before. "You've already accepted your fate?"

Dani tried for a carefree shrug and undoubtedly failed miserably.

"If I can prevent my death, of course I will and I know mom and dad and the Magicals will do everything they can to stop it. I know you will too. But the prophecy was written a really long time ago and I don't know if I have a chance to change my future. I definitely don't want anyone else becoming collateral damage trying to save me from something that can't be stopped."

Dani did not want to die. No one wants to die. But reality clawed its way into her head and made itself known. There was nothing that she or anyone else could do to stop a prophecy and change her fate. The only thing she could do was try to prepare as best she could for when the time came.
She would just have to be ready.

Chapter Eighteen

When Dani emerged from her bedroom the next morning the sun was up and Anders was gone.

Instead she was greeted by two other guards she'd seen in the courtyard upon her arrival who then explained that by order of her parents they were to her personal attendants until her guard returned.

"Good morning, sweetheart." The only brytlyn who seemed happy about this arrangement was Dani's father, the one who'd made it.

Dani gave a halfhearted smile. "Good morning, dad." She walked into the dining room with her temporary entourage in tow. There had been even more guards stationed downstairs.

"Slept well?" Her father clearly hadn't, but his mood remained unaffected.

"Better than I expected," Dani had collapsed on her bed the second she reached it but her night had been plagued by nightmares that left her shivering in a cold sweat and tangled in her sheets. All of them had depicted her final battle and in all versions she died a different way, none of them good.

Her father grinned. "Anders should be back soon with news of your security detail." That news wasn't nearly as reassuring as her dad wanted it to be.

Dani didn't hide her grimace as well as she thought.

"I know isn't ideal but your safety is my first and only priority. Nothing is going to happen if I can help it." His tone was so hopeful and determined that Dani almost believed him and she really wanted to.

That sobered her up a bit. "Whatever you think is best, dad." Dani amended softly.

"Don't worry, I talked your father down to only a few guards." Amandine glided into the room in a silk gown that glistened in the morning sun.

"Your mother thinks it best to not overwhelm you with a ten person team." Callan clarified, sounding like he very much disagreed.

Dani wasn't sure if she should be relieved to not be receiving a ten guard team or worried that her parents had actually considered it.
"How many guards am I getting precisely?" She took her usual seat, mentally trying to calculate the number of brytlyns

Elthorne could hold. They already had much staff and more than triple the guards.

Her father cleared his throat. "You will be starting with only one guard from the academy and more will be added in due time." He handed her a plate of pastries. "But your first guard will depend on who Anders thinks will work best with you."

Dani took a croissant and placed it on her plate. "Only one?" That number was much smaller than she had anticipated.

"Your mother convinced me that the transition will be smoother this way and I agree. You've only just begun to get comfortable with one guard shadowing you and adding a handful more may not be as beneficial as I believed last night."

"That's good." Dani agreed, picking apart her pastry. "But what about Will's security? Isn't it dangerous for both of us if people can just blink in here?"

"For now your brother's security will stay as is. Will isn't being threatened at the moment and I'm choosing to be thankful."

The heir to the throne wasn't in danger, the spare was. Dani found it incredibly ironic that her role was dangerous and came with more responsibility than being next in line to rule a realm.

She just nodded, pushing her breakfast around the plate with her fork absently. "How am I supposed to save a realm if I don't even know how to properly use my power?"

Dani wasn't bold like Delacour.

She wouldn't necessarily call herself a wimp but there were no circumstances in which Dani would've willingly challenged anyone in order to take back a kingdom. It was terrible to admit but all too true.

Callan cleared his throat, tearing her away from the frustrating thoughts. "The other sparker we mentioned prior will be your training instructor. Sir Hugo is very much looking forward to working with you."

Dani gave a distracted nod, far too wrapped up in her own fears to focus on much else. "Why do you think I was chosen for this?"

That was the question Dani had asked herself since the night before. Why out of so many Stallards before her had she been selected for such a burden?

Amandine pressed her lips into a thin, still line and folded her hands gracefully in her lap. "Perhaps the clairvoyant foresaw how similar you and Delacour would be? Handing such an intense power at a young age is no easy feat. It takes a very special brytlyn."

A sparker, evidently.

"I'm not that special," Dani refuted, putting her fork back down before her shaking hands threatened to do some serious damage to the poor pastry.

Her mother shook her head, a frown gracing her usually jovial face. "You are more powerful than you give yourself credit for."

"I agree," A very rumpled Will entered, his hair barely combed and tunic slightly crinkled as if he had changed quickly.

Dani grinned at her twin brother. "Good morning to you too,"

He sat in his usual chair and stole a pastry from the plate. "What have I missed?"

"We were just debating on why I was chosen to save Breckindale," Dani said, pressing her hands together as they gave off a brilliant red glow.

Will nodded, chewing thoughtfully and then swallowing. "Maybe you aren't supposed to figure that out yet?"

The suggestion created a ripple like a stone thrown into a glassy lake. It also gave Dani an idea that led to her spending the better part of her day researching in her room and studying her medallion like it held the answers to the universe. Maybe it did.

Dani hadn't been chosen for her position out of a random draw; she was completely sure of it and if a key did exist then she would have to find it. Her book was still being held captive somewhere in the palace but her medallion was on her desk, and as well as having her name and new title on it there was one more detail that struck Dani as not quite a coincidence.

The Ruby Savior

The eagle.

Chapter Nineteen

"What exactly are you looking for?" Anders narrowed his eyes at her from his spot near her open bedroom door, managing to watch both the hall and his charge at the same time.

Dani stared up at him from her spot on the floor, surrounded on all sides by books. "Something that ties an eagle to Breckindale's dark ages."

Her bodyguard nodded, eyes still narrowed in confusion. "I assume there is a reason behind this?"

Anders didn't quite look at her like she was crazy but he looked wary of her odd activity. To be fair, it was odd to be sitting in the center of a circle of book stacks that slightly concealed her due to their height.

Dani held up her medallion. "This has to mean something,"

There had to be a reason she'd been given a gift after her book was delivered and it certainly couldn't have been a coincidence that the organization Delacour had fought against mentioned

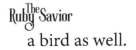

a bird as well.

"I very much agree," Anders nodded pointedly, giving her a look. "However, I don't believe that lugging half of the royal library into your bedroom is the right way to figure it out."

"I didn't bring half the library," Dani mumbled, eyeing the towering stacks of books all around, fencing her inside a circle of yellowed pages and gilded spines.

Her bodyguard didn't look convinced. "When I arrived at least fifteen guards were carrying ten books each for you."

"They offered to help me with my project so I asked them to give me any books that might discuss the dark age or Delacour," Dani explained. "They were very helpful."

Anders reluctantly nodded his agreement. "Have you found anything worth looking into?"

Dani shook her head. "Not yet, but to be fair I've only looked through six of them." There were at least a hundred surrounding her and they all had more than four hundred pages each.

"As your bodyguard, I am at liberty to inform you that you most definitely should rest before your first day of school tomorrow. Scouring through books can wait."

"But this is important," Dani promised. "You spent hours inspecting brytlyns at the military academy." Her guard had only returned fifteen minutes before.

"To find you a bodyguard," He reminded her pointedly. "And I truly think you'll like who I've chosen; she happens to be a very skilled warrior."

"She?" Dani looked up from the book open in front of her. Her expectation of a bodyguard had been a clone of one of the dozen of the soldiers downstairs with the same serious expression Anders wore like armor.

Anders nodded. "Libby is very excited to meet you, she'll be arriving in a few days,"

"Do you think I'll like her?" Dani still wasn't thrilled about the extra bodyguard idea, but maybe Libby wouldn't be so bad.

"I do, she reminded me quite a bit of you actually and she's received top marks at the academy so I trust her to keep you safe."

Dani smiled. Maybe she wouldn't mind having another bodyguard, especially one that was like her.

"What happened here?" Will poked his head in through the doorway. "Why did you take half of the library inventory hostage?"

"I'm researching," Dani replied, watching her brother grimace. "And just because you despise books doesn't mean they aren't useful."

"I don't despise them, I'm allergic to them." Will corrected, stepping into the room carefully as if the circle of book stacks could hurt him.

"That's ridiculous," Dani chided, grabbing a red and gold book from a stack behind her. "No one can be allergic to reading."

Will nodded insistently. "Well I am!"

Dani blinked her eyes. "No, you're just dramatic."

"And you're just mean," Will shot back, though he was suppressing a grin. "What are you busy researching?"

Dani held up her medallion again and pointed to the animal. "This golden eagle,"

Will's eyes widened. "An eagle is worth summiting yourself to the torture of reading all of these books?"

"Evidently," Anders muttered. Dani glared. Her guard wasn't helping her case.

She stared up at her twin brother, giving him her best and most dazzling smile. "Do you need something?"

"Yes," Her brother nodded. "To save you from yourself." He eyed the books as if they were a ticking bomb ready to explode around her at any moment.

"I'm perfectly safe in my book circle." Dani promised, sweeping her arms around her collection.

"More like a book cage. Can you even get out of it?"

"Yes," Dani told him, standing up and stepping over one of the smaller stacks far more gracefully than she'd expected.

"Point taken." Will held his hands up in surrender. Then his smile dropped and his somber expression made him look more like Anders's twin then her own. "You think the eagle means something?"

"It has to," She said, her green eyes meeting his narrowed ones, prompting her to continue. "The note and the present were given by the same people so I thought that if I learned more about the eagle I would learn more about who's behind it."

"That's logical," Anders nodded approvingly, looking slightly less concerned than he had only a few seconds earlier.

"Surprisingly, I agree." Will admitted, a grin reappearing on his face just as fast as it had left.

"You're surprised that I'm the logical one?" Dani raised her eyebrows at her brother's suggestion. He may have been four minutes older but she was at least two years more mature.

Anders disguised a cough as a laugh. He must've not been the greatest actor though and Dani could hear his failure quite clearly.

"Yes I'm shocked." Will muttered dryly, moving out of the way before Dani could hit him. "Kidding, I'm kidding! Your plan

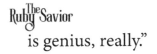

is genius, really."

"Thanks," Dani conceded, settling back down into her circle and picking up where she'd left off on research. Much to her confusion and shock, her brother followed, crouching down beside her and picking a book off of the closest stack.

"Can I help you?" She asked warily, uncertain on why her brother was now touching the thing he was claiming to be allergic to.

"No, but I want to help you." Will corrected brightly, scanning the book pages intently.

Dani narrowed her eyes at him. "With research?" Had he not just given her a long lecture on the horrors of books?

Will nodded, looking serious again. "Your research might help you figure out more about why you got chosen to be the savior and if that's the case then I want to help you with it. You were pulled into a prophecy and it wasn't fair."

Dani wanted to argue that none of this was really fair but she stayed silent.

"So partly because I'm really interested and partly because I don't want to even start thinking about school, I'm going to go through all of these books with you." Will promised.

Dani gave a fake pout. "It isn't because I'm your twin and you love me?"

"Well yeah but you already knew that part." Will said. "And I really want to help you. So whatever you are planning to do, I'm in."

"You're in?" Dani checked. "Even if we have to go through all of these books and the rest of the library?"

Will grinned, excitement brightening his green eyes. "I'm in."

Chapter Twenty

"I look like a blueberry." Dani tugged at the ridiculously puffed sleeves of her navy blue blouse viciously.

"You'll get used to it," Anders promised. "Everyone at the school has to wear a uniform just like yours and Will's." He took the bag leaned against Dani's bed frame.

Today Dani would be starting at Crystalium and her stomach felt too much like a butterfly sanctuary to be excited about it. Sparks had been shooting around her bedroom ceiling for ten minutes already and her shaking hands showed no signs of calming down.

"Is it selfish to worry about not making friends with everything going on?" Nothing had been resolved since the note was found. The Magicals had started an investigation but yielded no answers and Giselle still hadn't gotten back to Dani about their meeting.

The night before, Dani and her brother had been able to get through about twenty of the books she'd selected but had learned absolutely nothing. There didn't seem to be any connection between Delacour and an eagle or really anything about an important eagle in Breckindale's history at all. She hoped later they would be able to find at least something useful.

Anders shook his head firmly. "Outside of this mess you are still a teenager who's allowed to be worried about normal teenage things."

"But I'm not a normal teenager." No normal teenagers already knew when and how they would die.

"No, I suppose you are not but you never were anyway," Anders said. "Regardless of any prophecy you are still a royal, being just like regular brytlyns has always been out of the cards since even before you were born."

That helped a little, though the butterflies in her stomach never stopped. A fresh wave of panic was met with a fresh wave of sparks, flying high above her to circle her muraled ceiling.

"I'll be so behind in all of my classes," Dani realized. No matter who her parents were, the instructors weren't just going to pause their lessons and explain everything to her because of where she'd been raised.

Anders put a steadying hand on her shoulder. "No one will hold that against you, your instructors will be more than aware of the situation I promise you that."

"Okay," That eased some more of the panic clawing at her fearlessly.

"And tutors can be hired if needed." Her bodyguard promised.

Dani nodded. "Good," She would definitely need them if she wanted to pass any of her new subjects. She had never brewed a potion and she certainly didn't speak languages of magic animals.

"Well then they will be arranged, but for now you need to take deep breaths and calm down. I don't think your headmistress will appreciate sparks whizzing around her school." He gave the smallest of smiles, which Dani managed to shakily return.

"I don't know how to make them go away," She mumbled, closing her hands into fists in an attempt to block out the light they were radiating.

"Deep breaths," Anders repeated. "Just take a moment to just let yourself calm down while I go check on the security plan for today." And then he walked into the hall and shut the door.

Anders had talked Callan and Amandine into allowing just general security at Crystalium instead of giving her a full escort until Libby arrived. Her parents had agreed on the terms that it would give her an easier school experience and the headmistress had agreed to having a few of Elthorne's soldiers patrol during the day.

Dani walked over to the large windows that took up one of

her walls. The sun hadn't fully risen yet, giving the dark sky streaks of pink, a brighter blue, and a muted orange. She let herself just stare out the windows and focus on nothing but the grounds in her view.

A few minutes later when her door was knocked on her hands were at their normal temperature and her ceiling was clear. Dani had been expecting someone to enter, but instead of her bodyguard that someone was the very energetic future king.

"Ready for your first day of school?" Will asked, matching in the uniform he'd worn when Dani had arrived in Breckindale days before.

"Yep," Dani refused to let her brain focus on anything but the excitement it had long ignored. She had always looked forward to her first day of school every year, and now she got to have a magical do over. This was supposed to be fun.

"And dad told me you'll be getting your schedule from Sir Lechin when we arrive."

Dani really was excited about that part. Hopefully she would either be in a group with Everett or Eldridge so she would have someone to talk to.

"When are we leaving for that?" Dani knew Sir Lechin would be meeting with her before school to talk about her schedule but she hadn't been told how early they would be leaving.

"A few minutes," Will answered. "We should head downstairs

soon. Are you ready?"

Dani nodded. "Anders has my bag."

Will grinned. "And Leo has mine. Good thing our guards can't leave without us, they have all of our stuff."

And then they headed down the twisted maze of upstairs halls. Will kept a steady stream of conversation as they walked, doing a good job of keeping Dani away from overthinking everything.

Finally when they reached the balcony Dani spoke up asking, "You think I'll like Crystalium right?"

To which her brother confidently replied, "You'll love it." And then led the way down the marble staircase where their butler and two bodyguards were waiting. Callan and Amandine had been in an early meeting with the Magicals when Dani had come down for breakfast and were evidently still in one now.

"The jewels," Grantham opened an ornate silver box with different gems nestled inside their own compartments.

"Thanks Grantham," Will said, grabbing two and handing Dani one of them. Anders and Leo already had theirs in their hands.

"Ready?" He put his arm out and their guards did the same.

Dani wasn't, but it was far too late to say that now so she

nodded and added her arm to their semicircle. She gripped the small stone in her hand tightly, repeating the destination over and over in her mind before crushing the stone easily.

A flash of bright light illuminated everything and before Dani could even put her hand down she was whisked away to her first day of brytlyn school.

Chapter Twenty-one

"Why didn't you tell me our school is a giant glass castle?" Dani couldn't help staring up at the glittering archway as they walked under it, heading for the school.

At least three dozen towers jutted upwards, whilst the entrance itself was the size of a football field. Four large staircases were in view as the group made it inside and Dani peered around, taking in every view she could. The first floor seemed to never end, accumulating halls left and right.

"Did I not mention it?" Will grinned when Dani's eyes grew five times as large. "Pretty awesome right?" Awesome was the understatement of the century. If this was where Dani got to spend five days a week, school was going to be her favorite thing in the realm.

She watched the sun streak higher, sending shimmering streaks of light around the floor and walls. "Our school is a literal palace," Dani had thought Elthorne was the most gorgeous place she had ever seen but Crystalium even had her palace beat.

"Is everything in Breckindale shiny?" She asked, still looking around, eyes darting in every direction.

Will nodded. "More or less," Pride radiated from his smile.

Dani felt proud of the realm too. Her realm. The realm she was supposed to save from whatever evil would be terrorizing it in a few years.

"Stop." She intoned, forcing the thoughts away to continue staring at the glass infrastructure all around her.

A melodic voice interrupted the blissful calm of the academy, echoing through the glass hall. "Wilfred, how nice to see you!" The voice belonged to a shorter woman with blond hair and a deep skin tone.

"Hello, Headmistress Athena." Will greeted politely, moving to stand beside Dani again. "I would like you to meet your newest student."

"You must be the Dani I've heard so much about, it's very nice to meet you." Headmistress Athena gave a blinding smile. "Welcome to Crystalium Academy!"

"It's nice to meet you too," Dani replied, returning the smile. She liked her new headmistress already, who was a breath of fresh air compared to Giselle's alter ego.

Her headmistress nodded at Will. "Sir Lechin is in his office already so feel free to head down whenever you're ready."

"Thank you," Dani and Will said at the same time, looking at each other startled. Once their headmistress flitted away they started the trek down the hall.

Their bodyguards followed silently behind as Will led the way down the long main hall and then stopped at a door with a golden nameplate and emerald furnishings. It showed no signs of being occupied.

Dani approached the door carefully. "Do I knock?" She turned back to her brother and their guards.

Will gave a knowing smile, not looking particularly concerned. "He'll know we're here."

Dani didn't get to ask what her brother meant before the door swung open, revealing a man with coffee colored skin and wise eyes.

"Your brother is correct, Miss Stallard." Sir Lechin spoke calmly, his voice deep but clear.

"Hello, Sir Lechin." Will waved, completely unfazed. It was a far better reaction than the shocked one Dani was trying to hide.

The school advisor gave a papery smile.

"Good morning Will, you are here early."

Will nodded. "It seemed like a waste to come later when Dani had to come early already."

"I see," Sir Lechin switched his gaze from one twin to the other. "Please come in." She did as instructed followed by Anders of course.

Sir Lechin's office was painted in rich, cool tones that complemented the royal blue and silver bookshelf lining one wall. He had a neat oak desk with stacks of scrolls neatly tied closed with ribbon on one side and glass baubles on that other.

Dani took a seat in one of two leather seats opposite the desk, behind which Sir Lechin sat in his own leather chair studying her inquisitively. Anders stood behind her, arms behind his back watching both the door and Dani all at once.

"Welcome to Crystalium Miss Stallard we are thrilled to have you join us here." Sir Lechin leaned back in his chair, narrowing his eyes at her, though not unkindly.

"Thank you, sir." Dani replied, keeping the unease out of her voice while her mind spun trying to figure out what power he possessed that allowed him to sense them outside his door.

"I've put you in the platinum pod as its schedule is similar to your brother's though you'll find that the work ratio is a bit more manageable. Every year one pod gets the short end of the stick when it comes to mixing and matching class order and unfortunately this year it was the gold's." He handed her the top scroll with pearly white ribbon.

Dani unfurled it, glancing down at her schedule. She had history that morning followed by cipher in the afternoon with lunch in between.

Tuesdays were for her sparker training and physical education session while Wednesday was taken up by speech and the study of foreign species. Thursdays were a repeat of tuesday and friday was filled with elixirs and then stars and constellations.

"Congratulations on manifesting by the way, you and your brother were two of the first in your year to get your powers. Oddly enough another pair of twins manifested before you as well. I believe you know Everett and Eldridge Callisto?"

"I know them," Dani confirmed.

"I'm not sure if you know the other pair of twins who manifested the first month of school though." Sir Lechin glanced at her to check.

Dani shook her head. "The only brytlyns I know that are my age are my brother and the Callisto's, sir."

Sir Lechin nodded. "I figured, you have quite a large grade though I'm sure you'll meet them eventually."

Dani nodded, unsure of what to say. Thankfully the school advisor wasn't finished.

"I do apologize about your training room. It is in the north tower instead of the south tower like some of the others but your power requires a larger room and the ones in the south tower tend to be smaller."

"That's probably best," Dani agreed, reminding herself that her parents must've told him her power when she had been registered.

Sir Lechin smiled. "I trained in the north tower as well during my time here. It's the best in my opinion."

Dani smiled politely. "What's your power, sir?"

A part of her wondered if he was a sensor like Everett and had been able to detect their auras but she wasn't sure if that was possible through a closed door. The same logic disputed her theory of him being a transferer, since she didn't know if solid objects affected the reading of thoughts.

"It's a power nearly as rare as yours, Miss Stallard. I don't suppose you've ever heard of a clairvoyant?"

The word hit Dani right in the gut and made her hands start to warm. She wondered if Anders had picked up on it as well.

"Clairvoyants can predict things in the future." Dani told him, earning an impressed nod.

"Very good," Sir Lechin praised. "There aren't many new ones that manifest each year but it truly is an extraordinary power. Though it can be intimidating at times."

"If you don't mind me asking sir, how does it work?" Dani wasn't about to pass up an opportunity to learn about a power that had affected her life just as much as his own.

"Well most times I get flashes in my mind of scenes that will happen only moments later—hence why I knew you and your group were out in the hall without you knocking. Sometimes the flashes I get are of scenes that happen later in the future, though those are quite rare. And when I touch certain objects I can see images or scenes where they will be important, though those aren't fully formed in most cases."

Dani absorbed the information as best she could, nodding along as he explained.

"And what about prophecies?"

Sir Lechin narrowed his eyes and leaned forward in his leather chair once more. "Those are quite rare as well. Where did you hear of a prophecy?"

"I read about one in an old book from my library." Dani hated lying, though her excuse wasn't really a full lie. She had actually learned of a prophecy from a book in her library, there was just a lot more she didn't say.

"I've only studied prophecies during my school years but they usually put the clairvoyant into a dream-like state and give them very detailed scenes and intense flashes of the future."

"They seem very interesting." Dani observed quietly.

"Prophecies are quite fickle things," Sir Lechin said. "I'm sure the one you heard about was quite intriguing."

Dani nodded. "It was, sir." He just had no idea how much.

Chapter Twenty-two

"Welcome to another week at Crystalium Academy!" Headmistress Athena called, smiling at the impossibly large audience of students all in dark blue uniforms.

After her meeting with Sir Lechin had ended, students had begun entering the now brightly lit castle so they had headed straight to a large chamber the size of Elthorne's ballroom which was supposedly called the Hall of Guidance to await the rest of the students for the morning announcements.

Their bodyguards had brought Dani and Will to the side of the hall but close enough to the front that they weren't surrounded on all sides. Students had started whispering as soon as they saw the princess and they hadn't ceased until the Callistos had joined the twins and blocked out the stares.

Dani was well aware that she was the subject of all of them.

Some kids had mentioned how she had come from earth, some mentioned her age and wondered when she would manifest, some expressed concern over the guards they'd seen outside, and some just watched her with wide eyes.

Dani had never thought she'd miss being invisible.

"I trust that you all had a refreshing two days off but now it is time to jump right back into your studies. We have just over a month before midterm exams take place and I plan to spend all of that time expanding your knowledge as thoroughly as possible. Your instructors have warned me that this next month will be very crucial and I am thrilled to see how you all perform."

Dani glanced at Anders with wide eyes; he just nodded and gestured back to the stage.

"Now, I'm sure you have all noticed our new security situation as you entered this morning and I would like to put your minds at ease. This is strictly a cautionary measure put into place for the safety of one of our students and does not require rumors or whispers that I am ordering to end right now." The headmistress was so firm in her order that the whispers did cease though everyone stopped watching her and brought all their attention to Dani like she was being spotlighted.

The princess kept her head down.

The headmistress took a calming breath before speaking again. "I believe that is all I have to say this morning. Have a great day young brytlyns!"

Before the last word had even been spoken Anders and Leo

led the group out a side entrance and away from the hundreds of students going out the opposite way.

"You got your schedule?" Everett asked as soon as they were out in the hallway. Will was animatedly chatting with Eldridge a few feet away while Bree watched, an amused expression on her face.

Dani nodded, handing him the scroll. Her smile fell when he frowned.

"You aren't in my group or Eldridge's but we still have lunch together so that's good." He didn't stay upset long, a bright smile appearing back on his face. "At least you don't have potions first this morning, my instructor is always so grumpy."

Dani couldn't hold in her laugh when Everett straightened his back and twisted his face into a scowl.

"This way!" Anders announced, leading the group towards a small glass door and opened it, revealing a smaller staircase of metal.

Secret staircase?" Dani asked, nodding approvingly at the brilliant camouflage.

"Private staircase," Will corrected, letting his guard go up first and then following. Dani was right behind him the whole way up.

"Awesome," Dani breathed, turning to grin at her friends

climbing behind her. When they reached the landing the boys and Bree had to split, though they promised to see her at lunch.

Will stayed behind to help her find her first class, holding her schedule like it was a map.

"Is my instructor nice?" Dani asked, hurrying to keep up with her brother.

"Lady Imelda?" Will checked, not looking back.

"No, Iris." Dani replied dryly, though she did earn a smirk from Anders.

"I like her," Will said. "She's just a little strict."

Dani was used to strict teachers. She'd had many over her many years of human schooling.

When they turned and reached a long hall of tinted purple glass Will finally turned back. "My class is in the next hall over but I'll see you at lunch, okay?"

"Bye," Dani waved her brother off, feeling slightly lonely as he rushed out of sight. She still had Anders but after spending so much time with her twin it felt wrong to be alone.

She spun to face her guard. "Do I really have to go in there?" Without her ever confident brother, Dani felt some nerves flood back, though thankfully not enough to create sparks.

Anders nodded, a thin smile appearing on his face. "Yes you must go in, your royal highness." He said her title so loud that students passing by turned to stare.

Dani gave him her best death glare in return. "That was just cold." Even though the headmistress had stopped the whispers before, they started back up again leaving her with no choice but to enter her classroom with little enthusiasm.

Other students watched curiously as the princess took one of the open seats nearest the front of the room. The room didn't offer much of a difference from the classrooms Dani was used to except for all of the gold, silver, and glass scattered around.

"So you're the mysterious long lost princess?" The boy beside her grinned, his gaze mischievous.

Dani didn't like how her brain instantly compared him to Brendan. They had the same confident grin.

"You could say that," She replied, trying to play the polite princess her parents would want her to be. She was tempted to roll her eyes at him instead.

The boy furrowed his brows, looking genuinely confused. "You don't look like a reptile."

Dani grimaced. "Why would I look like a reptile?"

The boy still looked confused. "Isn't that what earthens are?"

"Humans," Dani said evenly, "Look just like brytlyns do."

"Huh. Sorry, I heard some of the older kids talking about them earlier and one of them said that they thought that since humans didn't have magic that they eventually shrivel up into tadpoles."

Dani shook her head, softening her steely expression. "Nope, they do get old though."

"I guess you'd be the one to know." The boy said. "We don't learn much about humans here but I always thought they were pretty cool."

"They are," Dani agreed. "And they have some pretty cool gadgets."

The boy paused, considering what to say next. "Do humans learn about us?"

"I didn't know brytlyns existed until I got here," Dani told him. "I still don't know too much."

The boy instantly brightened, his grin returning. "Well then I guess you'll need a tutor!" He spoke so loudly and caught her so off guard that it took Dani a moment to realize he'd just offered his services.

"Thanks," Dani said, "But I already am getting a whole team of tutors to bring me up to speed on these subjects, I don't really need one more."

The boy shook a strand of pale hair off his forehead. "You do realize we have all the same classes right?"

"So I've been told," She straightened immediately when a woman who Dani assumed was their instructor entered the room.

The boy didn't deter easily. "Well, you'll still need a friend, right?"

Dani did want a friend. "It wouldn't hurt," She said, voice kinder.

The boy held his hand out. "Amery Varron," He said.

Dani smiled. "Dani Stallard," She shook it.

Chapter Twenty-three

Dani survived her first class better than she'd anticipated and not just because Amery helped her with finding certain chapters in their insanely thick textbook.

Once she had found the chapters the assignment was a piece of cake. Dani had always been good at reading comprehension and writing notes didn't bore her to death like some of her new classmates.

Even Lady Imelda seemed impressed with her work, giving approving nods while she walked around the room. Unfortunately, the praise only improved Amery's opinion of his decision to help her and made him even more insufferable.

Dani couldn't claim she knew much about her realm and Amery did help but he couldn't be serious for more than a minute and chose not to use her given name.

"How did you like your first class, Mystery?" Amery asked, the lunch chime still ringing. He had apparently reached the conclusion that the name Dani just didn't work for him and had been calling her Mystery for the better part of class.

Anders found it terribly funny.

"I enjoyed it," Dani said, walking beside him and their group down the hall. It was no different then the history classes she had taken before except that her ancestors were the main topic instead of founding fathers.

"It's an interesting class," Amery conceded, turning back to face Anders. "Did you like it, Lieutenant Bower?"

"It was a very enlightening lesson today, Lord Amery." Dani's bodyguard replied, sounding perfectly at ease talking to a boy Dani had only just met.

"You two know each other?" Dani asked, confused. "And you're a lord?"

Amery nodded. "Yes to both questions, Mystery." The glare she gave him could have withered flowers.

"My official title is Lord of Hindley," Amery said, growing serious as they walked. "And since we are a part of the nobility I go to Elthorne often for ceremonies or balls and know some of the guards."

It clicked right then that Dani had talked to his mother at the reception. Though when she had told the duchess that she hoped Amery was in her group she hadn't met him yet.

"Lieutenant Bower is a really cool bodyguard, Mystery, you're lucky to have him." That may have been the first thing they had both agreed on the whole morning.

"I know," Dani promised, holding in her glare. She was grateful that she had such a great bodyguard but she didn't need the Lord of Hindley to tell her that.

Amery clearly didn't see the looks she was giving her amused guard when he wasn't looking. "Do humans eat food?"

"Yes, Amery." Dani knew he had said he didn't know much about humans but even that was an easy question. Didn't every living thing require a source of energy?

"But they still die faster?"

"Yes, Amery." Dani answered patiently. "But that's not because of food, it's because they don't have any magic to slow down their aging."

Amery nodded, pondering the answer. "Did you fit in there even if you weren't a real human?" That was the only question that couldn't be answered by two words.

And unlike the others, this one didn't have a definite answer. Dani had fit in as a human hadn't she? No one, not least her, had thought she wasn't a human and she'd lived there for thirteen years.

But that was scratching the surface on top of the whole mess.

That led to the truth that Dani didn't feel comfortable sharing to a noble boy she had just met. The answer would have been no.

Dani sucked in a breath, her hands shaking slightly. "I fit in much better in Breckindale." She admitted, thankful that for once Amery didn't press.

"The princess has done exceptionally well since her move." Anders affirmed, a pace behind them. Dani shot him a grateful look.

"I don't doubt it," Amery agreed, his smile sincere.

Dani gave the smallest of smiles back, searching for a subject change that didn't make her sparks flare up. "So what's cipher class like?" She really was interested to hear what the brytlyn version of math was like.

Amery faked a gag and comically rolled his eyes back into his head. "Horrible Mystery, truly awful."

"Lovely," Dani muttered, watching Amery pretend to fall asleep on her shoulder, adding extra weight as they walked. At least he was somewhat entertaining.

The lord abruptly awakened from his false slumber. "Kidding, it's not that bad if you like formulas and tables and charts. Do you?" He practically jumped down the stairs once they reached them, making Dani have to rush down while trying not to trip and fall.

"I guess so," Dani hadn't minded math at any of her old schools and wasn't half bad at it either. She really liked solving puzzles and that was more or less what math was about.

"I'm sure that will serve you well, Mystery." Amery decided finally as they approached a room the size of Elthorne's enormous foyer. Inside she could see rows of glass tables and cushioned chairs, each inside what appeared to be glass orbs that reminded Dani slightly of tents.

To her left were tiny glass buildings that students were lined up near and a shimmering glass chandelier that dropped from the ceiling.

"Incredible," She breathed, eyes trying to take in all the views at once. There were simply too many to take in.

"Just wait until you try the food here," Amery grinned, "I can personally guarantee it's at least ten times better than anything you had on your old planet." Dani doubted anything could top a brownie sundae but the excitement on his face made her hopes soar.

He beckoned her over to the line and waited until they were inside the first glass building before giving her a lecture about the best sweets he was piling high on both of their trays.

"You'll definitely need fudge cakes and bluroos," Amery placed what Dani could only describe as a thick chocolate cake with sprinkles and cream as well as something that resembled a multicolored donut on her tray.

She wasn't able to get any other word in before he placed more odd foods on her tray as well as on his.

He must have mistaken her surprise for doubt because Amery said, "Don't worry, in a week you'll be a pastry connoisseur." and then took both of their trays and ran off with them to the other side of the cafeteria.

Dani glanced at Anders who was holding in another laugh. "Are you going to let him steal your food?" He grinned and looked out the glass walls to watch Amery sit down at a table.

"No, I guess not." Dani sighed, giving her a bodyguard a pointed look and rushing off to the table.

This was going to be a very interesting year with Amery Varron.

Chapter Twenty-four

"So you survived?" Will checked, sitting on his bed and flipping though one of the many books covering his floor and desk.

They had returned from crystalium less than an hour before and to the shock of Dani, her twin had insisted they start research right away.

"Like you said I would," Dani conceded from her spot on the spotless rug, a thick leather bound book laying open beside her.

Will shot her a triumphant glance. "You should listen to me more often. I have brilliant ideas."

"That's debatable," Dani retorted. "Very, very debatable. But school wasn't as bad as I thought it would be."

It had actually been fun. Amery had been right about the food being amazing, though Dani wasn't sure that eating so many sweets every day was healthy, a concern she had voiced at lunch where she had been rebuffed by Will, Amery, and

Everett.

Will had been offended for sure but his two best friends had declared it their personal mission to teach her the wonders of brytlyn sweets until Dani rebuked her horrible healthy ways. They had then pretended to dramatically faint when she told them that they were ridiculous and that Eldridge was the only normal one out of the four of them.

Cipher also hadn't been as horrible as Amery had implied. Some of what the class was learning was similar to the trend lines and scatter plots that Dani already knew, giving her an advantage when it came to understanding the subject.

It had also been hilarious when she had realized what low tolerance their instructor had for the young lord's antics, though Amery either didn't notice or paid it no mind.

Will sighed, frowning. "I'm glad you liked crystalium, but I promise you my ideas are truly brilliant. When my ideas will help the realm, you'll see."

Dani looked back up from her book. "I'm sure that they will. That's what the king's job is right to help the realm."

"And to lead it and protect it," Will huffed, puffing out his chest and keeping his chin high.

Dani shrugged, returning to her research. "I'm pretty sure that last part is my job actually."

Silence followed loud and deafening. Dani's joke landed but it landed far harder than she would've liked.

"Brytlyn schools are different from human schools." Dani noted, flipping to and reading another page that wasn't the least bit helpful. Although most of it was interesting none of it gave any insight as to why an eagle was on her medallion and how it related to Delacour.

"I figured," Will said, eyes on his book. "From what you told me I'm sure Crystalium is realms away from what you were used to literally." He snickered at his own joke.

"No kidding," Dani countered, the conversation with Amery earlier seeping back to the forefront of her mind too vivid to ignore.

Coming to terms with the fact that she had never belonged on earth was harder to accept than anticipated. Dani knew she wasn't human and shouldn't have ever gotten on their world but it still made her heart squeeze tightly in her chest.

Will closed his book abruptly, the sound getting Dani's attention. "Are you excited for training tomorrow?"

"I am," Dani replied. Her sparks made her uniquely qualified to save an entire realm and she really wanted to know why. Hopefully learning how to properly use the power that made her so special would give her insight.

"I think you'll like our physical education session tomorrow too. Is there something like that on earth?" Her brother asked, switching out his book for another with a dark green cover.

"Technically yes but I'm sure it'll be different," Everything else in Breckindale seemed to be.

"I'm guessing humans don't learn how to vanish? I'm pretty sure that's what we are doing tomorrow."

"They don't have magic, remember?"

"Of course I remember," Will scoffed. "That's why you were able to move there in the first place."

His words made another question move into Dani's mind, one she'd never thought of before.

"Why doesn't earth have magic, Will?"

Dani didn't know how many other realms existed other than Breckindale but she doubted any of them were magicless like earth. If they were closer to Breckindale and had no magic then Dani would've gone there instead.

Her brother seemed to consider the question for a few moments of agonizing silence. "I don't know," He said finally. "I don't think it's ever been explained."

To Dani that definitely felt strange. She made a mental note to ask her parents about it later once they had finished with their advisors. At the very least Giselle would probably tell her.

"Yeah, Giselle would know." Will agreed, not even trying to hide that he'd used his power on her.

Dani nodded. "I have a lot to ask Giselle," Her meeting had been promised but no date had been given yet.

"I'm sure the meeting will be soon. The Magicals have just been really busy here lately." Will didn't state the reason nor did he have to. Dani knew the Magicals were spending every moment at Elthorne to find a way to stop her prophecy.

But the very thought made Dani wonder if it was the right thing to do.

She'd suspected earlier that her note had been a warning to prepare her for what would come in the future. The writers must've thought it was necessary or they never would have taken such a risk at the guarded palace.

Dani wondered if the note had been so cryptic for a reason. One that she didn't quite understand.

But maybe her medallion was the key.

"There are the kids!" Callan grinned as he and Amandine entered, both in full regal garb. He wore a dark uniform full of medals with a dark blue sash from his right shoulder to his left chest. Amandine wore a royal blue gown covered in diamonds and silver embroidery.

"How was school?" Amandine asked, kneeling beside Dani,

careful to avoid the books around her.

Dani smiled. "I love it!" It was different then her old school but much more exciting.

"I'm glad you had fun," Her mother beamed. "I'm sorry we weren't able to see you off this morning. Our meeting ran longer than expected." She shot a meaningful glance at Callan.

"Did the Magicals make any progress?" Even if talking about her new responsibilities made her stomach churn, Dani hated suspense much more.

"Not as much as we'd like," Callan muttered. "But it hasn't been very long." He added the last part after Amandine gave a reassuring nod.

Dani chewed her bottom lip. "Are they going to announce why we have more guards?"

"Not yet," Callan shook his head, staring intently at her. "Unless you want them too?"

She didn't. "I think it's better if we keep that between us," The less people who knew, the less weird Dani would seem.

"They did announce the new date for the winter ball." Amandine announced, lightly changing the topic.

Will's eyebrows shot up. "When did they move it too?"
"Sunday evening, they decided that due to all of the

circumstances, having it as soon as possible would be best." Callan said, the smile he wore not quite meeting his eyes.

Dani's stomach filled with butterflies and her hands grew warm, a red shimmery coating seeping around them.

If the Magicals thought that the ball needed to be in six days then what did they fear would happen after that?

Chapter Twenty-five

Dani really hated stairs. Especially when there were multiple narrow flights and the air seemed to thin with every landing they reached. Naturally, it was only a fact she realized when she had to pass those exact obstacles to reach her training room at the very top of a tall tower.

She didn't think she was out of shape physically but by the time Dani reached the fourth flight Anders offered to carry her up the rest. She refused in order to keep what little dignity she had left and regretted it all the way up. Her bodyguard wasn't even breathing hard.

This was going to be a big problem twice a week.

"Do elevators exist in Breckindale?" Dani grumbled, her legs throbbing and chest heaving.

Anders raised an eyebrow. "Elevators?" The way he repeated the word slowly was all the answer Dani needed.

"They are big metal platforms that go up and down," Dani explained, half climbing and half dragging herself up what she hoped was the final flight.

Her heart leaped when a very ancient silver door stood to the left of a creaky landing that had clearly seen better days. It looked like something straight out of a Halloween movie.

"Interesting technology humans have," Anders muttered, helping her up the last step and moving beside the crystal wall to the right of them. Dani sucked in a shaky breath and knocked on the door before she could chicken out.

She of course couldn't wait to meet her sparker instructor and to start training but something about meeting the only other living sparker was daunting and made her fidgety.

"You may come in, Miss Stallard." Only a moment had passed since she had knocked, and with a final glance at Anders, Dani did as her instructor said.

Her instructor turned out to be a tall man with short hair and wrinkles that made him appear older and wiser than any other brytlyn she had met so far, even Sir Lechin.

"Hello," Dani said.

"Hello," Sir Hugo replied.

"You must be my new student," Sir Hugo smiled warmly. "My only student ever, I'll add." He chuckled.

Dani liked him already.

"There aren't dozens of Sparkers to teach at this school?" She gave a wiry smile that made him laugh even more.

"Just you," Sir Hugo gave a rueful one in return. "Which conveniently leads us into our first topic of today's lesson."

Dani raised an eyebrow until he continued. "I know just as well as I assume you do that being a sparker requires far more training then a sensor or even a winder would need. The power calls for constant control over one's emotions which as a teenager may be significantly more difficult but not impossible."

Right on cue Dani's hands began to shake, this time not with anger or fear but with hope.

"So I can control my sparks?" Dani didn't want a repeat of her manifesting experience ever again. No matter what Iris assumed it had been absolutely terrifying.

Sir Hugo nodded, no doubt hidden in his expression. "With time and practice of course you can."

That may have been the best news Dani had heard in her entire life.

"So I wouldn't just randomly shoot sparks everywhere?" She checked, the news feeling too good to possibly be true.

"Not unless you command them to," Sir Hugo answered, his lips tipping into a smile when Dani's eyes lit up.

"I can command my sparks?" She had been considering her sparks free spirits that go wherever they wanted and do whatever they chose. They sure acted like it.

Her instructor nodded carefully. "With practice you'll learn to," Eldridge had said that if Dani learned to take control of her power she wouldn't be so against using it and she hoped he would be proven right.

"But first I'd like to teach you a skill that you will hopefully enjoy." He moved to the center of the room putting his hands out in front of him, palms turned out. Before Dani could even blink her eyes green sparks started spinning around him like a tornado, covering him head to toe in sparks.

Dani's brain screamed at her to move back but her feet refused to listen, forcing her to stay frozen as she watched the sparks slowly start to fizzle out as Sir Hugo resurfaced.

"What was that?" She finally willed the words out once Sir Hugo turned back to face her, looking completely calm and unscathed.

"That," he smiled patiently, "Was a spark sphere. A very simple and beneficial skill that you are about to learn."

Dani had never willingly created sparks before. "What do I do?" She asked, her hands still shaking with energy.

"Our power pairs with our emotions but works in different ways with each emotion. For this skill I'm afraid the emotion you will need to utilize is fear in order for the sparks to react and act as a shield."

Dani nodded, getting it in her head that the sparks were protecting her. Defending her from everything outside.

"Why don't you try it?" Sir Hugo moved back, giving her the middle of the floor to create her spark sphere.

Dani gave what she hoped was a confident nod, closing her eyes to concentrate. "Sure," Fear was the easiest emotion for her to utilize and within five seconds she already had a list.

Being the savior scared her.
Having to defeat something evil scared her.
Her family being in danger scared her.
Dying terrified her.

When she opened her eyes again a steady stream of red sparks were flying out of her hands and starting to ascend around her, circling slowly at first but gaining speed as more joined.

For the first time Dani was glad to be a sparker.
Amazed.
Proud.

She felt powerful.

The fear was instantly replaced with joy and the sparks

disappeared as quickly as they had come, giving one final rotation before fizzling out completely.

When her sight wasn't blocked by spark, Dani saw Sir Hugo clapping and Anders nodding proudly from the hall.

"Incredible," Her instructor commended, "It took me weeks to form a spark sphere and I was far older then you when I tried." Sir Hugo seemed stunned at her display. "Your control truly was impeccable."

Dani beamed. Her sparks had always done their own thing and left her scrambling to pick up the pieces. This time had been different. This time she didn't have to scramble for control, terrified her sparks would hurt someone or cause damage.

"We should see what else you can accomplish." Sir Hugo decided. "You seem to be quite a natural when it comes to harnessing your power."

The comment both made her smile widen and her stomach fill up with dread. Dani was definitely proud of her control and of her spark sphere but those same things also confirmed the clairvoyant's predictions with tremendous accuracy.

She could be as powerful as Delacour had been.

Dani had foolishly thought that if she turned out to be horrible at using and controlling her power then there was no way she could do anything with it, not least save an entire realm. Apparently she could do near impossible things by barely trying.

But the clairvoyant had been right about everything so far and prophecies weren't made to be broken.

And if her power was even more powerful than expected then she really was the savior after all.

The savior who was completely and utterly doomed.

Chapter Twenty-six

That afternoon Dani made the executive decision to see Giselle herself.

The idea struck halfway through her sparker session but was only proven even more necessary during her physical education training when to the surprise of both instructors, her classmates, and even herself, Dani vanished for an hour and forty eight minutes and broke the school record.

And now hours later she was standing in front of a large manor adorned with pink stones and an archway labeling it Briarwood. Dani had only been allowed by her parents to visit if Anders and two other guards accompanied her for safety.

She realized halfway through knocking on the door that she hadn't asked Giselle if she could come or told her that she would be dropping by. But it was a little late now and her favorite Magical did not look happy as she rushed to get to the door.

"Iris I swear if you don't—" Giselle paused when she saw Dani, the frustration plain on her face melting into concern. "What are you doing here?"

"Things happened at school today," Dani answered simply, letting Giselle lead her into the shiny mansion where everything was either blush pink or cream.

The woman finally stopped in a large sitting room with plush chairs and a window that practically poured light inside. "I take it those things weren't good?"

Dani couldn't tell if Giselle had used her power or not when she took a seat in one of the chairs and invited her to do the same.

Dani shook her head. "I did really well in sparker training today and then vanished for an hour and forty minutes during physical education."

Giselle smiled proudly. "Dani, that's amazing!" Her smile dropped when the girl shook her head again. "Why isn't that amazing?"

"Because it means the clairvoyant was right," Dani said the words far louder than she meant to. "I'm just as powerful as Delacour was." She really wished she wasn't. Not in these circumstances.

"That's not a bad thing," Giselle promised. "Being powerful shouldn't be viewed as a bad thing." She repeated.

But to Dani it wasn't just bad, it was proof that her fate was sealed. Her destiny was already written and had been for a long time.

She deflated in her seat. "It means that I'm the savior for real, Giselle. It means there was no mistake after all."

The hope Dani had been desperately clinging to dissolved away, leaving her empty with despair and disappointment.

Deep down she'd known trying to evade the truth wouldn't help anything. No matter how hard she had tried to convince herself otherwise, a golden medallion laying on a stack of books in her bedroom proved her delusions false. As did the note in the book Dani still hadn't been given back.

"As opposed to it being fake?" Giselle spoke the words like they pained her. "You're the savior whether you like it or not. Whether any of us like it or not." Dani had no doubt that if she could Giselle would have stopped the clairvoyant behind the prophecy and given him a hefty glare until it was changed.

"My dad seems to think it can be avoided if I have more protection," Dani said quietly. Elthorne was more like a military base than a palace at this point, with an abundance of guards in every hall and entrance.

"Your father is a smart man, Dani. But even if he wants to deny it he knows that you are the savior and he knows what the title entails. He is just trying to protect you from the outcome of the job." Giselle's voice faltered and even though she wasn't the transferer there Dani knew exactly what she was thinking about. The one thing Dani herself had tried not to think about for the past few days.

"My death."

Giselle nodded. "But it won't come to that. None of us will let it come to that." She looked so determined that Dani almost believed her confidence. She really, really wanted to.

"But I'm only one person. How am I supposed to fight something or someone prophesized to go against the realm and beat them alone?" Delacour had at least been brave enough to fight back. Dani was a coward.

Giselle sucked in a breath before her lips formed one word. Another one came out instead. "You're not alone in this."

Now the princess was confused. "But guards can only shield me from physical threats." Dani was the target, not Anders and Libby. They couldn't save her from a magical fate predetermined so long before.

Giselle seemed torn on what else to say so instead she stood and walked over to the wall to her right. When she placed her left hand in the middle of it a panel popped open, revealing a small square chamber that looked like it was made of metal. Giselle pulled a scroll of parchment out of it and calmly walked back to her chair.

Dani stayed glued to her seat, watching with wide eyes.

"I wasn't referring to your bodyguards, Dani." Giselle replied, unfurling the scroll just enough for small dark words to be visible.

Small, dark words in the same handwriting as the note written in Dani's book.

Ruby The Savior

Chapter Twenty-seven

"Technically I'm not supposed to show you this per the instructions of your parents and the rest of the Magicals," Giselle warned warily. "But I for one believe you deserve to see this regardless of security concerns. We read it earlier yesterday morning and I think you need to read it now. "

That didn't make Dani feel much better.

But she did take the scroll and unfurled it completely, the message written in familiar dark ink making goosebumps appear on her arms and legs.

Dearest Savior,
It is an honor to extend our warmest congratulations
on your newest title.

This order was created to aid the former savior and
in accordance with her final wishes following the
discovery of a prophecy regarding both of you to
assist you and do whatever we can to thwart the end

*of the prophecy like we could not with Delacour. To
find us, follow these instructions as soon as you are
allowed.*

Fandvorl Aste Traecenn

Dani put down the scroll to stare at Giselle. "The instructions
are just gibberish!" Fandvorl Aste Traecenn didn't even seem
to be real words.

"I know," Giselle sighed. "And it's not in any of the languages
spoken here if you were wondering. Cordelia tried and failed
to translate it yesterday."

That dashed the one idea Dani had been able to come up with.
She had wondered if any of the dialects in Breckindale were
a match for the instructions considering how many she had
seen in the language textbook she'd found in her backpack
before her first day of school. They all had duplicate syllables
and far too many curled accents for Dani to even try to speak.

"What about my medallion?"

Giselle arched a perfect brow. "The gold one we found outside
Elthorne?"

Dani nodded. "I've been trying to figure out what it means.
I thought the eagle on it could have been a clue or a hint or
something. Maybe the instructions are another one."

Adrenaline raced through Dani's veins like bursts of energy

in a circuit. She liked puzzles that made her calculate and consider all angles in order to solve them. The challenges enthralled her.

The most important puzzle of her life was laying there in her hands.

Hearing she had backup made everything she'd learned about the prophecy sound far less overwhelming. Reading the words made her feel less alone then she had ever felt.

"You would know better than any of us," Giselle replied softly.

"Mom and dad really wanted to keep this from me?" Dani kept her gaze fully on the scroll but she could tell Giselle was weighing her answer.

The decision was most likely more her father's than her mother's and Dani was sure of it. Callan was trying to protect her from all types of threats now it seemed to her.

"Only for a little while," Giselle broke the uncomfortable silence. "They still feel you haven't had enough time to properly adjust to everything yet."

They weren't wrong in that assumption. Dani knew that. She also knew that her mom and dad had already lost her once and didn't want to lose her again, this time permanently. Dani didn't want to lose them either.

In less than a week she had found out that she had magic,

had spent her entire life being raised by strangers, moved to a magical realm, met her real family, gained a bodyguard with another on the way, started school, and had gotten integrated into royal life. And now Dani knew that a secret society was trying to save her life thanks to orders given by her dead predecessor.

"Were they waiting until after the ball?" The palace had been even more chaotic since the announcement that the winter ball was taking place so soon but everyone was much more excited than before.

"That was the original plan," Giselle confirmed gently. "And I would advise you to keep quiet from them that you have the scroll. Wilfred as well."

"My parents wouldn't want me to have it," Dani filled in, running her fingers along the edges of the scroll. She knew her mother and father must've had a good reason for not showing her the scroll but the decision didn't hurt any less.

This was a chance to fix her destiny. The only chance.

"The choice was not made lightly," Giselle promised. "But the king and queen's first priority will always be the safety of you and your brother."

"My parents think that not giving me the scroll that is promising to help save my life is protecting me?" To Dani it made no sense.

"They do not wish to ignite false hope for themselves or for you."

Dani pressed her lips into a thin line. "Maybe hope is exactly what I need,"

Giselle gave the tiniest hint of a smile. "They do believe in you," She said softly. "And so do I."

Chapter Twenty-eight

"May I advise you to perhaps not lie to your mother and father?" Anders stood guard near the doorway of Dani's bedroom, scanning the hallway for threats.

They had barely been back for three minutes and Dani's bodyguard had spent the entire one hundred and eighty seconds questioning her course of action.

"I'm not really lying," Dani looked up from her notebook just long enough to see him staring at her cautiously. "I'm just not telling them the full truth."

She wasn't thrilled about it either but once her supporters were found and the whole prophecy mess was solved Callan and Amandine would be grateful to have a daughter who wasn't going to die instead of mad that she had deceived them.

Anders was the only person Dani had told and the only one she planned to.

"The exact action you told me made you mad at them in the first place," Her bodyguard spoke calmly, not a hint of emotion in his voice.

He had a point and Dani knew it.

"Giselle was just trying to help and I don't want to betray her trust." That was only a half truth. The other half involved Dani not wanting her scroll to be confiscated like her book had been.

Anders crossed his arms over his uniform. "So you aren't hiding the scroll in your desk drawer to avoid it being taken away?" He grinned when she glared. That was exactly what she was doing and it apparently wasn't as brilliant as she had thought.

"I just need some time to solve the riddle and then I promise I will give the scroll back to Giselle and tell my parents," Dani said, her pencil moving furiously across the page.

"Good, but perhaps you should move the scroll to a better spot that is harder to access?" Anders suggested, giving the desk drawer a side eye.

Dani narrowed her eyes. "Where would you suggest?"

Anders glanced around her bedroom. "The back of your closet? Behind your dresser?"

"But I like having it in my desk drawer so I know I won't forget it or lose it. And I did hide it under a bunch of other things." Dani said, making another quick note in her notebook, the tip of the pencil pressed onto the page.

She had copied the clue down into one of her notebooks so she could start cracking it but so far the only progress Dani had made was that it was indeed three words. The meaning of them was still unknown and Dani was frustrated like never before.

"This makes no sense!" She scratched out another scrawled note on her page. There were several.

Her head of security just watched. "Have you tried any of the languages on earth?"

"The words don't look familiar," Dani didn't know the majority of the languages spoken on earth and she was the one who was supposed to solve the instructions. The organization behind it had to have known that amongst so much they knew already.

She would have elaborated further but a dark haired teenager in a dark blue uniform strode in before she could. "What words don't look familiar?" Will asked.

"Dani was just reading a chapter for her history class." Anders shot her the slightest of grins.

"It's very confusing," Dani agreed, shutting her notebook. "What's up?"

Will looked confused. "Aren't we doing more research?"

"Actually I was thinking we could start again tomorrow after school. I have some homework to do tonight." Dani told him carefully.

Her brother shrugged. "Okay, I was thinking of going exploring in the dungeon anyway. And mom needs to see you in her office. I think your gowns for the ball are here."

"Thanks," Dani couldn't resist being excited about ball gowns. "Have fun in the dungeon."

"Have fun with your homework," Her brother grinned, dashing back into the hall and out of sight before Dani followed with Anders by her side.

"There you are, darling!" Amandine smiled warmly when Dani entered her office a few minutes later. "How was your meeting with Giselle?"

"Fine," Dani replied, eyeing the ribbon-covered boxes sitting on her mom's desk.

Amandine stood to move beside her. "I know you have plenty of gowns already in your closet but I wanted you to have a few special ones for balls and galas." She lifted the top off of the first box with red ribbon, holding up a lavender gown with silver embroidery and pearls dotting the bodice.

"It's beautiful," Dani breathed, gently reaching out to feel the light fabric.

Amandine's smile only grew. "When I attended my first ball after getting engaged to your father I wore a lavender dress and I always said that if I ever had a daughter she would wear a lavender dress to hers too but i got a few more choices in case you wanted options."

Dani shook her head. "I love the lavender one, mom."

And she really did, but more importantly it was the one her mom had chosen and wearing it felt indescribably right.

"You haven't even seen the blue one yet," Her mother cautioned, folding the lavender one and placing it back into its box carefully before unwrapping the one beside it and pulling out a baby blue dress dotted with silk flowers and small diamonds.

The blue one was just as gorgeous but Dani wasn't going to wear it to this ball. Her heart was already set on the lavender one. "Maybe I can wear that one to the next party," She said.

"Are you sure?" Amandine asked, now putting the blue one away and moving on to the box in the middle of the row.

Dani nodded, eyes still locked on the first box. "Positive."

And she was still positive three pastel dresses later when her mother asked the guards stationed near her hall and Anders to bring the boxes back to Dani's bedroom for her.

Dani couldn't tell if her mother looked more touched or elated when she repeated her decision on wearing the lavender dress and then followed the dress entourage back to her bedroom. She stayed out in the hall when they dropped the boxes off and then thanked them as they dispersed back to their stations, or in Anders' case to his usual spot in her doorway.

"Don't say I didn't warn you," He muttered once all other guards had left their hallway.

"What?" Dani questioned, waiting for her guard to elaborate. He didn't say a word, just calmly entering her room and pointing.

In the direction that her guard had been pointing to was Crown Prince Wilfred of Breckindale, the scroll in his hand.

Chapter Twenty-nine

Exploring a dark, creepy dungeon had never been on Dani's bucket list of things she wanted to experience in her lifetime yet here she was walking in a line with her brother, his bodyguard, and Anders while trying furiously not to run away.

After Dani had scolded her brother for snooping through her stuff and then making him swear he would keep her scroll a secret she let him explain how he had found it.

Will had explained how he'd just wanted to borrow a piece of paper for his history homework after being reminded of it because of Dani's fake excuse so he rummaged through her desk to find one and ended up finding and then reading her secret scroll.

He then had decided that in order to hide the scroll from their parents it would need a much better hiding spot in a much more secluded place in the palace which was why the two of them and their loyal bodyguards were busy exploring the darkest and deepest corner.

"Why did you have to choose the dungeon?" Dani groaned, crossing her arms and keeping them close to her as they walked.

Will held a lantern up, illuminating the large space and himself in yellow. "Because mom and dad aren't likely to go in here and it's the coolest place in the entire house.

Dani shook her head so hard her hair whipped against her face. "No it isn't, it's creepy!" She recoiled when her voice echoed into the darkness.

"You wouldn't think that if you'd gone exploring with me before," Will grinned, the light making him look extra scary.

Dani turned away to instead face her bodyguard. "It's creepy now and it would have been creepy on Saturday."

"You wouldn't have found it less creepy if you knew where we were heading?" Will asked incredulously.

Dani shrugged. "Maybe, but I trust you to find a good hiding spot for the scroll and then after that I'm out of here,"

Will laughed. "Deal. We hide the scroll in the perfect spot and then you and Anders can leave,"

Anders didn't seem scared at all, no hint of emotion on his face. He'd mostly stayed silent during their trek to the dungeon except to promise Dani that there weren't actual prisoners down here, much to her relief.

That relief had vanished the second they had actually reached the dungeon and a half dozen spiders had skidded across the floor, leaving Dani to hide herself behind her bodyguard in a sheer state of panic.

"Thank you so much," Dani retorted, keeping her eyes narrowed in an attempt to try to see better. It didn't help much in the dim darkness. "Where are we going anyway?"

"To the dungeon hallways," Will answered, continuing down the long hall they had been following since they'd entered.

"Isn't that where we already are?"

"No," He acted as if Dani's answer offended him deeply. "This is just the entrance hall. In a few feet it splits off into a few hallways for the cells and other rooms down here."

"Lovely," She muttered, peering around into the darkness that was only growing into an abyss ahead of her.

It took everything in Dani not to scream and head back the way she had come. She had to remind herself over and over that this was for her survival. This was important. The reminders helped a little but the second she remembered that she was indeed in a dark dungeon with bugs and dust the bravery faded instantly.

It was a miracle that she hadn't accidentally formed a spark sphere yet.

"Here we are!" The Crown Prince announced, holding his lantern high, illuminating the hallways that branched out on all sides of them. "Ready to explore?"

No. Dani was absolutely not ready to go explore creepy hallways. She just stared at her brother blankly.

Will didn't seem to notice. "That's the spirit!" He gleefully went into one hallway on his left side, followed dutifully by Leo. Dani reluctantly took one to her right, though she made Anders go first.

There weren't any people in the cells they passed.

The walls were a dim gray and the doors were wood. Dani hated it. She was scared enough to create a flurry of sparks that danced above her hands but not enough to make a spark sphere. She was okay with that.

Instead Dani focused on her goal, looking around for a hiding place that wouldn't be easy to overlook in case she needed to find her scroll but also one that wasn't too obvious. The cells were out of the question and besides them there was little else in her hallway.

"This was not a good idea," Dani wrinkled her nose as red light brightened the very dirty cell wall. She wondered if anyone had ever been held there. Maybe during the dark ages?

Anders didn't agree nor did he argue. "Your brother is right though, your parents haven't been down here in quite a while."

That was a good thing but it didn't come close to outweighing the negatives of this experience. There happened to be several.

"Are there any other rooms in the palace my parents don't venture into?" She asked hopefully, switching the position of her hand to gain a better view of the wall.

"Not many," Her bodyguard answered. "And none of them have opportune hiding places."

The fact that the best chance happened to be at the very bottom of the palace in a large dimly lit space was frustrating. Unfortunately the dungeon had been a genius suggestion from her brother, even if Dani really wanted to disagree.

"Dani, I found something!" Will's volume was loud enough to echo his message a few times over as Dani hurried back to the hall he had picked. Anders stayed by her side.

"What did you find?" Dani couldn't see much else other than her brother, their bodyguards, and a chest that he was holding in his hands. It was intricate and covered in dusty diamonds.

On the top was a name. That name was Delacour.

"That's her, right?" Will glanced at Dani. "The last savior?"

Dani nodded. "I'm Delacour's heir," She said the words softly, though still loud enough for all of them to hear.

The chest was longer than it was wide; the scroll would fit in

it perfectly.

Anders stared at the chest skeptically. "Where exactly did you find this?" He asked Will.

"In the room at the end of this hall. I went in there to find a hiding spot for the scroll but I found that instead. It isn't a cell either, it's like a sitting room or an office or something."

"What?" The dungeon wasn't falling apart but it wasn't in the greatest shape either. A sitting room in the dungeon made no sense.

"I'll show you," Will promised, leading them to the end of the hall where a heavy wooden door stood, no better than any of the others for the cells.

But when he pushed open that door a cream colored, well lit room was behind it. A circular oak table stood in the center, its gold rim sparkling. The marble floor was pristine.

"What is this?" Dani wondered, completely shocked that a room this nice could exist beside run down and endlessly dirty cells.

"A sitting room or an office," Will repeated, circling the room to inspect everything in it.

Dani did the same.

The room was furnished comfortably but was simple compared

to any of the other rooms Elthorne boasted. Other than the table there wasn't much to look at so she turned her attention to the engraved chest, opening the lid carefully.

Inside there was a pair of pearl earrings and a crumpled piece of paper lying on top of black velvet.

Dani unfurled the paper first.

"Never fall if you can spare a jump," She read the note out loud, the words in cursive and written using dark ink.

"What?" Anders who had been standing guard near the door moved to stand beside her. Dani could see he was ready to unsheathe his sword.

She held it out to him. "This was in the chest. I think Delacour may have been the one to write it."

Anders didn't say anything else he just took the chest from the table and ran his fingers along it, inspecting every inch.

"I don't think that's the only thing in there, Dani." Her bodyguard said, his finger on a set jet black crystal hidden among the velvet.

His words brought Will jogging over, his eyes twinkling with curiosity. "What else is in there?"

Dani narrowed her eyes at him but didn't say anything. Of course her brother would be excited about a secret chest in a secret room in a spooky dungeon of their palace.

Anders pressed the stone down and the velvet popped up. Dani forced herself back when Anders and Leo removed the velvet and got to the chamber underneath, pulling out something round and gold.

Dani stopped breathing.

"It's just like yours," Will glanced at her, the smile wiped from his face.

It was. The medallion was gold and round and had an eagle on it.

The only difference was the name.

This one had Delacour's name where Dani's would have been though the title underneath stayed the same.

"I think it is best if we let your parents know about this." Anders told her gently, still holding the medallion.

Dani's mind was spinning too fast to attempt an answer. She had thought the puzzle was simple but with every new piece that got added the notion kept seeming more and more untrue.

"Maybe there is something I can learn from it?" She croaked out the words, confusion and dread still pooling inside her like a river.

With every piece of the puzzle things just got more complicated, more difficult, and certainly harder to understand. But Dani still wasn't sure that this was the last piece left to find.

Chapter Thirty

"Why are you doing school work during lunch, Mystery?" Dani didn't miss the interest in Amery's voice as she got out her notebook. It was Friday afternoon and although all other brytlyns were eating lunch and chatting, the young princess was scribbling in a notebook.

Dani glanced at him from over the page. "Just trying to get ahead," She said the lie as nonchalantly as she could with her limited acting skills.

Truthfully, Dani had spent every night since finding the medallion researching Delacour and compiling a list of everything she'd learned. Her findings added up to one page of a mini biography beside the page Dani had devoted to the clue from her scroll.

Amery furrowed his brow. "In what subject?"

Dani felt incredibly rude to be writing while at lunch with her friends but Everett and Eldridge hadn't arrived yet and neither had Will. Until they did she was going to make as much progress as was possible.

"History," She reused the excuse she'd given Will days before.

This time Amery didn't argue or tease her, he just nodded and went back to his food. She'd been worried that if he ate so many sweets he would get sick so Dani had forced the young lord to pick one fruit and one vegetable from the line. So far he just picked at them and grumbled complaints.

"Mind if I sit here today?" A blond haired girl asked, plopping down beside him.

Amery sighed. "You usually sit with your own friends," From the way he was grumbling Dani was pretty sure they knew each other.

The girl gave a matching glare in return. "Well I haven't officially met Dani yet and I felt like having lunch with you and the boys today.

Amery frowned but didn't argue. "Dani, meet my lovely twin sister Lydia."

"Nice to meet you," Dani said, returning her amused smile when Amery stabbed a pastry in defeat.

"We are going to be best friends, I just know it!" Lydia's tone was cheerful with just a bit of Amery's confidence mixed in.

"You two got here early today," Will said by way of greeting as he and the Callisto twins approached the table. "Hey, Lydia."

It took Dani a moment to realize that her table was made up of noble twins. She found that amusing.

"That's because someone made us sprint the whole way here." She explained, glancing with narrowed eyes at a now very innocent looking Amery Varron.

"Well someone was hungry today!" His stomach had growled through the last hour of class and due to the way the desks had been positioned, Dani had heard it the entire time. "And we didn't sprint the whole time, Mystery."

They hadn't, only because Anders had constantly warned them to be careful and Amery respected him enough to listen.

"What are you working on?" Eldridge asked, eyeing her book a split second after she closed it.

Dani met Will's eyes and attempted a carefree smile. "I was just trying to get ahead on my work so I have less to do before this weekend. Plus I started etiquette lessons yesterday.

The excuse had been technically true but the real reason found its way back into her head, the unsolvable words taunting her.

Fandvorl Aste Traecenn frustrated her to no end.

"Etiquette lessons?" Everett raised an eyebrow.

"The ball is Sunday night and I'm not princess ready," Dani explained, her hands warming slightly with nerves. The party was so close now and the excitement produced a dizzying array of emotions.

"You'll love it," Lydia promised. "We all dress up and eat cake and pastries."

The mention of dessert brought over a young woman with long blonde hair streaked with pink. She wore a pink tunic with puffy sleeves and fitted dark pants with heeled boots.

She looked accusingly at Dani. "You didn't tell me there would be cake,"

"I didn't know." Dani promised, holding her hands up to further prove her innocence. "Everyone, this is my new bodyguard Libby. Libby, meet Everett, Eldridge, Amery, and Lydia."

When Dani had arrived home from Crystalium the day before, Anders had introduced her to her new fashionable bodyguard who had right away declared that they would be best friends just as Lydia had done. Dani believed it just the same.

"So these are the friends I got to hear tons about," Libby flashed them her bubbly smile. "It's very nice to meet all of you." And then she flitted back to her post opposite where Anders stood.

For Libby's first day at Crystalium she had been put on Dani duty for lunch following a lengthy patrol during the morning session where Anders had been with their charge. They had explained that both of them would be present for lunch and then Libby was fully in charge of Dani during her final class of the day.

Eldridge frowned. "You got more guards?"

"Just Libby for now, more are coming later."

"Why?" Everett asked. "Did something happen?" He glanced at Will as if expecting his best friend to introduce his new guard as well.

Dani wanted to tell them everything. She wanted to start from her move to Breckindale and fill them in on every single detail she had learned since, including the book, her medallion, the scroll, and the chest. She wanted to share her power and what it meant. She didn't like keeping secrets, even if they were necessary.

"Just a precaution,"

Lying to her friends made nervous butterflies soar in her stomach once more, her hands being coated with the red shimmer Dani had just about gotten used to. But she couldn't force any other words out of her mouth.

Everett looked suspicious but said nothing and Eldridge and Lydia either just didn't want to push or fully believed her. Only Amery's continued stare made her think he didn't and gave her a bad feeling she couldn't shake.

It all got too much.

A handful of ruby red sparks danced in her palm, only barely visible from above the table.

Will nudged her. "Dani," He muttered, "Breathe."

Everett and Eldridge already knew her power, so instead of staring at her with wide eyes like the Varron's were they glanced around the cafeteria to make sure no one else had seen what the princess had just created.

Dani obeyed, breathing in and out until the sparks dissolved again.

"What was that?" Lydia hissed, thankfully keeping her voice low.

"I second that question, Mystery." Amery nodded.

They deserved to know. They all deserved to know everything.

"I should probably start at the beginning," Dani decided weakly. And she did, she launched into a full story starting at her fateful math class and ending at her secret visit to Elthorne's dungeon.

She expected her friends to be completely in shock and have a gazillion questions for her but both pairs of twins were completely silent. When they did speak all four of them wanted to help. Lydia even wrote the code down so the four of them could start research after school while Dani and Will kept on reading their history books.

The relief that her friends didn't ditch her and the excitement that they were all doing a project together got Dani through the rest of her day.

And even an hour later when her potions instructor was droning on about a powder called weaklise and making the entire class take two pages of notes about its effects her good mood stayed. Only when she arrived back to Elthorne to a few of the Magicals in the foyer wearing dark expressions did it begin to waver.

Unfortunately for Dani things only got worse from there.

Chapter Thirty-one

Exactly five minutes after stepping into Elthorne's massive foyer Dani was trying not to picture herself as an inmate in prison.

She was seated on her bed while her parents and the Magicals formed a semi circle around her. None of the advisors present were ones Dani knew well and their expressions gave no hints of warmth. Her father held the scroll in his tight fist.

"Why didn't you just tell us Giselle gave you the scroll?" Her mom was far more calm then her father was at the moment but Dani was still slightly scared of her sharp tone.

Dani kept her head bowed. "Because I thought that if I did you would've taken it away before I could try to solve it." She was proud of how strong her voice sounded, especially with everyone's eyes zeroed in on her.

But clearly her assumption had been right.

Callan sucked in a sharp breath and closed his eyes for a moment before responding. "So your solution was to hide it in the dungeon instead?"

Dani had agreed with her brother that it was a good plan. They had even checked on it before and after school to be sure it was safe and secure.

"My plan," She replied, "Was to figure out the instructions written on the scroll. I hid it so it wouldn't be confiscated."

"I figured as much," He grunted. "Is trying to protect you too much to ask?"

"The scroll was addressed to me," Dani mumbled. "Protecting me from learning helpful information would have done nothing."

"Did it make you feel better about the position?" Cordelia asked the question like the conversation was an interrogation.

"Finding out I'm not alone in this?" Dani stopped herself from raising her voice. "Learning that I might have a chance to not die before I graduate school? Yes, it did."

"You were never alone in this," Amandine said quietly. "We have been working tirelessly to make sure the fate you mentioned doesn't occur." She didn't even want to repeat the word.

"There have only ever been two saviors in the entire history of Breckindale."

Dani had been told during her previous etiquette lesson that confidence was an important factor in getting a message across. She was confident that the knowledge she was about to share would make her audience listen.

She took a deep breath and then launched herself off the deep end.

"Delacour made the decision to end the dark age herself and save the realm, creating the position that has now been passed down to me. She saved everyone but herself. The prophecy terrified me when I found it and learning about what Delacour endured just made me feel all the more secluded. And since I'm guaranteed to follow in her footsteps of course it was relieving to know that I have people behind me who understood what I have to do."

The room flooded with silence, no one else daring to end it.

Even the king and queen whose only goal was to protect their daughter were speechless. Their daughter had just admitted that she felt alone in a palace of hundreds and trusted a group of strangers more than anyone else to help her survive.

Dani herself was comprehending the scary thought. She had never felt invisible in Breckindale but now she truly felt seen. Now she felt understood.

"Why didn't you come talk to us?" Her father finally broke the suffocating silence, his eyes and tone softer.

"I don't know," Dani ducked her head once more, letting her hair fall over her like a shield. "Maybe because I knew you'd react like this?"

The second the words left her mouth she regretted them.

They cut like a sword.
And then they drew blood.

"React like this?" Callan repeated, barely holding back the bitterness in his voice. "I just got you back after thirteen years." The words were so raw and cold that Dani couldn't force herself to look back again.

"I let two humans raise my daughter her entire life. Thirteen years that I could have been your father and that you could've been here with us all wasted because of the brilliant power you were foreseen to have. The role that the power gives you. The role that says it will be your demise."

Dani only flicked her eyes up for a second to see her mother lay a comforting hand on her father's arm before looking back down again.

She knew Callan's goal wasn't to make her feel guilty but she did just the same. She never should have said that she felt alone, no matter how much she'd meant it in the moment. It had stung and hurt her dad.

Dani had a family, two bodyguards that she trusted and friends. She was everything but alone.

But then why did you say that? Dani didn't even know the answer to her own question. The one she eventually came up with bruised her from the inside out.

She'd wanted to be understood.

Invisible girl.
That was what she had been on earth.
The shy girl with perfect manners and an intuitive head.

In Breckindale everything was flipped.
Here she was royalty. Known. Seen.
The mystery princess that everyone was wondering about.

And she was the savior.
A piece in a game Dani didn't know how to play.
She was Delacour's heir.
The girl who was doomed to die.

Her position was unique in a way that made Dani's stomach churn. The argument she had inadvertently started between herself and her father may have been wrong but everything in her speech had been the truth. Her truth.

No one but herself would completely understand the role she'd been chosen for. And Dani was even failing at that. She was failing a lot of things at the moment.

Maybe hiding the scroll had been a bad decision on her part. It had started this explosion that Dani had never meant to cause.

She had made a mess of everything just because she'd wanted attention. That was absolutely pathetic.

Even Dani had turned against herself at that point. And surrounded by her parents and their advisors all with stormy expressions all she wanted to be was invisible once more.

Chapter Thirty-two

That night Dani had asked Anders to bring up her dinner instead of eating downstairs like she had every night since her arrival. She did not want to face her family.

Once Callan had said his piece and Amandine had kissed her on the forehead they all left her to wallow in self pity.

Dani hadn't had the heart to try to solve any mysteries nor did she want anything to do with homework so she curled up in her bed and stared at the mural on her ceiling until boredom set in.

Her etiquette instructor Lady Silvia must've been canceled that day and Dani was glad. She would've wrinkled her nose at how blotchy Dani's tear stained face and rumpled her school uniform looked.

But Dani wasn't in the mood to care.

Her goal was to be holed up in her room for as long as possible.

She had everything she needed in her room and knew and trusted Anders enough to know that if she continued asking for meals he would deliver them.

And he did. "Here's your dinner," His tone was even when he entered and set the tray down on the desk that she cleared. Dani had moved the books so that she didn't have to look at them.

"Thanks, Anders." Dani was glad that her manners were still intact at least.

Her bodyguard nodded. "Your parents are worried about you," His tone betrayed nothing.

"In what way?"

Were they worried about how she was feeling or worried about the risks she was taking?"

"In all ways, I suppose." Anders clarified calmly. "They asked me to check on you."

Dani nodded once.
"How much did you hear?"

"How much would you like me to have heard?"

"All of it I guess," Considering Anders was one of two people Dani felt like talking to and the only one she had known longer than a day she needed his advice.

"Do they hate me?"

"No, Dani."

"Should they?"

"No, Dani."

"I shouldn't have started the argument in the first place." It was painfully ironic that she'd made such a dramatic statement about hating feeling alone whilst now sequestering herself in her bedroom and only talking to her bodyguards.

She looked to Anders, waiting for him to say something but he stayed silent. Dani wondered if he agreed and just didn't want to admit it. She wouldn't have blamed him.

"You have been through more change than most people go through the entirety of their lives." Anders finally spoke up, voice solemn. "And the entirety of your life has been completely changed without your knowledge nor consent and you have still taken it in stride."

Her life in Breckindale felt much longer than only a week. It felt like a lifetime ago that she had manifested.

"You of all people should be allowed to be frustrated about everything that has occurred. Although it may not have taken place in the best manner I believe neither your parents nor the Magicals are under the intent that it was done out of malice. I certainly don't and my entire job revolves around knowing and understanding your way of thinking so that I can protect you."

Dani released a breath she hadn't known she'd been holding.

"I didn't mean to lash out," She agreed quietly. "But I don't want to be treated like I'm incapable of handling myself."

Callan's words had impacted her more than she'd realized at the time probably because her emotions weren't clouding her judgment.

Dani had heard the reasons that led to her relocation but she had never taken a moment to think of how much pain her parents had gained because of it.

They had both gained and lost their only daughter in so little time, all while not knowing the truth behind the power that had torn them apart. Dani wondered if Amandine blamed herself as much as Callan did or if Will had ever asked why his twin sister had been taken away.

Dani had thought of herself as the victim when really she'd only suffered a sliver of the heartbreak. She'd grown up with a loving family in a good neighborhood. It sure could've been a lot worse.

"I don't think anyone questions your ability to handle yourself," Anders reasoned. "But you shouldn't have to, which is why you have Libby and I."

He waited until she met his eyes before continuing. "And I know you don't agree with his methods, but your father means well."

"I know," Dani mumbled. "His guard idea turned out better than I thought."

Anders managed a rueful smile. "I take it you like Libby?"

"I love Libby," Dani's new bodyguard had spent her free time giving her makeup tips and fashion advice. She'd really gained a twin brother and a big sister from her move.

"Just not the idea." Anders concluded, most likely remembering the numerous complaints he'd received from his charge.

Dani nodded. "And I do wish my information didn't get sent through a chain of command first."

"Another angle of protection," Anders explained, not sounding too thrilled about the tactic either.

"But how is keeping me ignorant protecting me?"

Anders seemed to be weighing how much to tell her, his normally steel expression flipping through emotions faster than a television could switch channels.

Then he broke the silence.

"Sometimes to protect those we care about, our course of

action is to shield them until we believe them to be ready." He said.

Dani nodded. And then she was left alone.

Chapter Thirty-three

Dani managed to continue her seclusion the entirety of Friday evening and well into Saturday morning. She had plenty to keep her busy until Libby delivered her breakfast and then kept her company while Anders patrolled.

And then on Saturday afternoon her seclusion came to an end with a knock on her door as Dani stood near the large windows that took up one of her four walls.

"Can I come in?" The deep voice on the other side was achingly familiar and belonged to the person Dani had been avoiding since the day before.

Her half baked plan had involved hiding away in her bedroom until the ball on Sunday night and avoiding her parents as much as possible during the event. It hadn't occurred to Dani that either of them would actually want to talk to her.

"Okay," She replied, staring at the door until it slowly opened and her father entered.

He gave a nod. "I take it this means you are being social again?" Dani couldn't tell if he was teasing or not, his tone betrayed nothing.

Seeing her father made all the regret from the day before surge back up. "I'm really sorry," Blurted out first. "For everything, dad."

"As am I," He said the words like he needed to be rid of them. Callan moved beside her, his gaze falling to the palace grounds running miles deep.

Dani followed his gaze but didn't face him.
"I shouldn't have hid the scroll from you and mom."

"Perhaps not," Her father acknowledged, still staring forward. "But I understand why you did and I'm so sorry." He finally turned to face her and Dani saw the regret plain on his face.

"For taking away my scroll?"

"For putting you in a position where you felt that you had to hide it," Callan corrected. "You were right about my reaction, Dani."

Dani did know that. Her father's one goal was to keep her safe.

"I've spent the last thirteen years blaming myself for not protecting you well enough and this is the result." Even if he tried to mask it, Dani could hear the hurt and shame in his voice.

"It wasn't your fault," Dani knew that even before the full story had been explained. "If I hadn't gone to earth I wouldn't be here now." She would have already been dead because of the enormity of her power.

Her dad didn't seem to see it that way. "I could have done something," The crack in his voice broke Dani's heart. "I shouldn't have let them take you away."

"I don't think there was any other option." Even if her power hadn't manifested right after her birth it surely would've caused problems eventually. It was now.

Callan had to clear his throat twice before saying, "Do you want to know the original plan we discussed?" The question was so abrupt that it caught the young princess off guard but she nodded nonetheless.

Callan took a deep breath.

"After we were told that earth was the safest place for you, your mother and I proposed that one of us would go with you and we would trade off every few weeks for Will. Our hope was that you wouldn't have to be alone there."

Dani shook her head so hard her hair whipped against her face. "You couldn't just abandon the kingdom."

"For you," Her father didn't continue until she met his eyes. "We will do anything." The sincerity in his voice shattered Dani's heart—but it healed it too. Callan wasn't angry at her at all; he was mad at himself for something he couldn't control. Dani hated that even more somehow.

"If I ask you to do something you'll promise that you'll do it?" Dani asked quietly.

"Anything," He agreed, just as she had hoped he would.

"Well then I don't want you to blame yourself," Dani said. "For any of it."

"Any of it?" He let out a bitter laugh as he repeated the words.

Dani wasn't going to give up so easily. "It was out of everyone's control except the clairvoyant who got the prophecy. I know the choice wasn't ideal but you and Amandine saved my life by sending me to earth and if you didn't then I wouldn't be here to get to know both of you and Will. I'm really glad I can now."

That quieted her father and Dani left him to his thoughts for a moment, just staring out the window silently, eyeing the grounds.

"It really wasn't my fault," Callan finally whispered, sounding like the thought had just sunk in and registered.

"No."

That one word seemed to lift the weight off of his shoulders and when he strangled her with a hug Dani felt herself relax as well.

"I love you, dad." Dani whispered it so softly she wasn't sure if it was even audible until he tightened his hug.

"I love you too,"

When he finally released her Dani let out a content sigh, grateful that things were fixed.

"Are you excited for the ball tomorrow?" Her dad's smile was as bright as the one Dani wore.

She nodded. "Very," And she really was, especially now that everything was back to the way it was supposed to be.

"That reminds me I'll have to teach you how to dance."

"Dance?" Dani narrowed her eyes to slits. Her father laughed.

"My father taught your aunts before their first ball."

"You want to teach me right now?" Dani's plan for the ball had been to talk to her friends and eat the cake Lydia had promised, not to dance and fall on her face.

"No," Callan shook his head, "Right now there are a group of young teenagers who urgently need to talk to you. I was told it has to do with your scroll."

Dani gasped. "They figured it out?"

Her father shrugged but he was smiling. "I guess you'll just

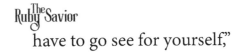

have to go see for yourself,"

Dani nodded, rushing off to the stairs as fast as she could.

"We did it," Amery grinned as Dani descended Elthorne's grand staircase, Anders and Libby only steps behind her. "We just figured out what your clue means, Mystery."

"You did?" Dani grabbed the paper Lydia had been holding like a trophy. On it were the three clues with the letters neatly crossed out and rearranged below until every line was crossed out minus the last.

Dani glanced back up at her friends, smiling. "It's an anagram." Of course it was. She had been looking for a complicated solution to the riddle without even giving a second thought to the old word game she'd played with her human parents at least once a week.

"At first we thought you were right and the clues had to do with Delacour so we invited Will, Amery and Lydia over to go through our library." Everett explained, eyes twinkling with excitement.

"And then we found absolutely nothing so I had the brilliant idea to go through some of the code books Favian keeps and we discovered the art of scrambling letters that humans like to do." Amery cut in, a triumphant smirk on his face.

"They weren't really common here," Will started, "But we thought it was worth a try because of its popularity on earth.

Clearly it was good that we had."

Dani nodded. It was great that they had.

The group behind the scroll really had thought of everything to ensure only she was able to solve it.

"So are we geniuses or what?" Amery's grin was even more smug than usual and this time Dani didn't even care.

"Yes, you're all geniuses." She promised. "What are the instructions now?"

"Frovland East Entrance." Eldridge finally spoke up, his expression troubled.

Dani carefully met his gaze. "Is that bad?" She didn't recognize Frovland but her friends clearly did and weren't thrilled about it.

"Difficult would be a better word for it," Lydia corrected.

"How is it difficult?" Dani wasn't sure why they looked so nervous now that they'd found the location. She could just blink there or take the coach.

Amery's smile dropped. "Frovland isn't in Breckindale, Mystery. It's a completely different realm entirely."

"It's another realm?" She frowned.

Everett nodded. "You have to use a special gemstone to get there, though that's not really the troubling part."

"Then what is?" Dani wondered, searching each familiar face expectantly.

"The gem stones only work every two nights." Lydia added cautiously.

Dani nodded, letting the words process in her head. "When was the last time that they worked?"

Will frowned. "Last night, Dani."

Dani nodded, calculating in her head.

"Okay so I can try tomorrow night, right?" It only hit her a second later that she couldn't.

"The ball." All five of them said together, their voices echoing through the palace.

Dani slapped her hand to her head. "I won't be able to sneak away at all!" On a normal night and with permission it would be a possibility but definitely not at a ball with hundreds of people crammed into the palace. She had no shot.

"No you won't," Anders agreed from the edge of the stairs. Dani hadn't known that he and Libby had been listening in on her conversation.

"You could always wait two midnights after that," Lydia suggested, and she wasn't wrong in that argument. Tuesday night would be more opportune than Sunday to sneak away.

"I think I'll at least try tomorrow," Dani decided firmly. "The sooner I can get to Frovland the better, right?" Her assurance was mostly for herself but the enthusiasm didn't sway the nerves stirring in the pit of her stomach. It didn't erase the doubt on her friends' faces or the frown on her brother's.

"Do you even know what you're blinking yourself into?" Libby wondered, making her way over to the group.

"Not really," All Dani knew was that her supporters expected her to get there.

And she would. She had to.

Chapter Thirty-four

By the time Dani made it outside the ballroom doors she could already hear the nobles chattering and the musicians beginning to play their instruments.

Her delicate lavender ball gown was gorgeous but the fabric did little to defend against the goosebumps covering her arms and legs. The weather had grown increasingly colder since the previous day and the constant opening of the double doors didn't help anything. Neither did the nerves apparently.

"You look beautiful," Her mother whispered, her midnight blue gown swishing around her. "But please remember to breathe."

"That's important," Dani agreed, releasing the breath she hadn't noticed was being held hostage. They would be making their entrance any minute now.

She hadn't realized how heavy her tiara truly was until it had been propped upon her head amongst the loose curls falling down her back. Dani couldn't tell if the tiara was truly weighing her down or the fact that when Grantham returned the family would be getting announced.

Anders, as her head of security was in charge of keeping her safe during her entrance and while she socialized. Libby was there in case Dani fell on her butt or tripped on her dress.

Her family's bodyguards had the same orders Dani's did: make sure their designated royal was safe no matter the circumstances. The rest of the guards stationed around the ballroom were in charge of the guests her parents had invited.

"Everyone is ready, your majesties." Grantham reported, meeting them just outside the doors. Dani had to remind herself to breathe when her father nodded.

Dani shuffled back, allowing her grandmother to pass in front of her and Will while her aunts and their families stood behind the two of them.

"Presenting King Callan, Queen Amandine, and the Queen Dowager of Breckindale!" Grantham boomed the words so loudly Dani's ears rang.

"Ready?" Will whispered, watching their parents and grandmother walk through the doors and into the ballroom as it flooded with thunderous applause.

Dani wished she could say no.

"Presenting, Crown Prince Wilfred and Princess Danielle of Breckindale!"

Dani had no choice but to put on a brave face and stride forward into the ballroom of brytlyns all dressed in finery and jewels. Five minutes later she had already shaken at least fifteen hands and met more titled adults then she could keep track of.

None of them were familiar, though Dani did spot Favian and Genevieve across the room at one point. Everett and Eldridge hadn't been with them, most likely with Lydia and Amery eating the desserts piled high on silver and gold platters like the other noble children in attendance. Dani wasn't so lucky.

She made her way through the masses, greeting the guests in front of her and making small talk until her father made his way to the center of the room and the crowd pushed back against the walls, allowing Dani to follow her mother and twin towards the king.

She knew her father was supposed to make his speech and that she was supposed to be listening but Dani's mind only strayed to her plan to get to Frovland.

The gemstone needed to successfully blink to Frovland was called a Frost Crystal and the one person in the realm who happened to have a collection of the rare stones was Dani's father who had thankfully given her permission to use a few. The plan itself was simple.

Get to Callan's office.

Get the crystal.

Blink away.

Do whatever has to be done in Frovland without missing the end of the party.

The steps echoed over and over in Dani's head only starting to fade when her fathers voice and hundreds of eyes staring at her brought her back to the present.

"First, I would like to begin by thanking you all for coming to the Winter Ball once again this year. As always it is a joy to open up our home and to be reunited with so many dear friends."

When the crowd clapped Dani clapped too, standing beside her father as he spoke.

"This ball in particular is one that my family and I will always look back on fondly and one that I sincerely hope my daughter will enjoy." He paused to smile down warmly at Dani, more applause echoing through the room as he did so.

"Now please enjoy the festivities!" As soon as the crowd swarmed forward Dani bolted as fast as could to the corner where Anders had been observing. Will followed, only a few paces behind.

"Have you seen them?" They asked together.

Anders nodded. "You passed by them a few minutes ago. I sent them to where Libby is standing to wait," He pointed to the closest exit where her blonde and pink haired bodyguard was waiting with four young teenagers— or more accurately the heads of four young teenagers.

"Go time," Will muttered, walking beside Dani as they threaded through the crowd as best they could until Anders cleared a path and they sliced forward and then to the right.

"There you are, Mystery." Amery may have looked regal in his new attire but the grin he wore was anything but.

"Ready to head to dad's office?" She turned to her brother first, letting him nod before she faced the others.

"Yep," Everett cheered at the same time Amery announced, "I'll lead the way!"

Libby crossed her arms and stared at the young lord using the most impressive glare Dani had ever seen her use. "I'll lead the way." She corrected, marching them through the nearest door and around the empty halls until they reached the expansive foyer and its grand staircase.

The four boys raced up first with Dani and Lydia behind them, holding onto the railings as their shoes clacked against the marble.

"Your turn, Dani." Will gave her a hand up to the landing while Amery helped his twin sister.

She nodded, taking a breath before hurrying down the hall, breaking into a wobbly sprint around the twisted maze of hallways until she found the door she was looking for and raced in.

On Callan's desk was an ornate silver box covered in etchings of symbols Dani didn't recognize. He had unlocked it earlier for her so the heavy lid opened easily enough, leaving an impressive dozen of pure white stones with blue stripes visible.

The chest was eerily similar to Delacour's, the deja vu making the dread fill up in her stomach as she pulled three out.

Dani handed one to Anders and another to Libby before she could second guess herself.

"Good luck," Lydia whispered, giving Dani a quick hug before stepping back. Her hands were in tight fists at her sides.

"Be safe," Everett said, his usually cheerful grin quivering slightly. "And please hurry back. If you leave me with Amery and Will too long the entire dessert table will be gone."

Amery and Will both nodded enthusiastically at the prospect.

"I'll keep them in line," Eldridge promised. "And guard the table with my life."

Dani almost smiled. "Good luck with that," Eldridge's job seemed almost as difficult as hers and at least twenty times as impossible.

"Be careful, okay?" Will hugged her even tighter than Lydia had, his green eyes betraying nerves Dani hadn't expected.

She nodded, tightening her grip for only a second before her twin pulled away and shuffled back to stand with their friends.

"Anything Amery?" Dani noticed that he was the only non traveler still with them.

"I expect a thorough update, Mystery." For once Amery stayed serious, only the tiniest hint of a smile appearing when he gave a mock salute and finally moved back, leaving only Dani and her protectors in the circle.

"On three?" Libby suggested as all three of them held the stones out. Anders waited for Dani to nod before nodding himself, giving Libby permission to start their countdown.

"One," She said.

"Two," Anders continued.

"Three," Dani whispered, and then together they crushed their gemstones and blinked away from the realm.

Chapter Thirty-five

"This is the east entrance of Frovland?" Dani had expected a gate or sign of some kind to mark the location but all she could see for miles was blue in varying shades.

"Evidently," Anders muttered, staring down at the bright grass under his boots.

Libby frowned and coiled a strand of pink hair around her finger. "Was that really their only clue?"

"Yep," Dani shivered, just as confused as her guard about their surroundings.

The grass was an electric bright blue, the sky was midnight with a contrasting white sea of stars and the trees were periwinkle and covered in a thin layer of frost that also lightly crusted the ground.

"This is where we are supposed to be,right?" Libby checked, arching an eyebrow like the color palette offended her.

="That's what the note told me." Dani mumbled, glancing around at her surroundings. No other brytlyns were in sight.

"Maybe try telling them you're here?" Anders put a hand on her shoulder as he drew out his sword with the other. Both he and Libby were assessing the empty forest for a threat.

"Sure," Dani agreed, cupping her mouth with her hand to be heard over the harsh wind.

"Hello?" She called into the deep forest of blue.

No response.

"My name is Dani, your clue brought me here!"

Still nothing.

It was barely midnight and the scroll hadn't given any specific deadline for her to solve the riddle. Dani wasn't wrong. But still, no secret society was appearing to give her answers.

"I'm the one your scroll was addressed to!"

The silence that followed those words only made Dani that much more frustrated.

Could the clue have been a cruel prank like Iris had thought? The very idea that Iris was right about something made Dani want to gag but this time she refrained only because it was necessary.

Had they been wrong about the clue?

And if they had, was all of her lying and hours of research for nothing?

Dani didn't even try to stop the sparks that started pouring out of her hands, letting them add flashes of light in the otherwise dark location.

"I'm a Sparker!"

A soft rustling from ahead made Dani's heart soar with excitement. She prayed that it wasn't her imagination.

The anagram was the only thing that made an ounce of sense when it came to the note, even if it had been gibberish at first. The organization behind it knew too much about her for a word puzzle to simply be a coincidence, not when she had played them so often in her childhood. Her friends had to have been correct; this was the right place.

"I'm the Savior of Breckindale!"

The noise grew louder and Dani almost cheered with relief.

She ignored the tittering of the guards behind her, evidently trying to convince her and each other of the best course of action. Both Anders and Libby were too focused on their debate to have heard the sound.

A crack of ear splitting thunder however did get their attention and with weapons drawn they moved closer.

It clicked in Dani's head barely a second later. The entire reason she had been chosen had been because of one person. The one person who had a medallion identical in almost every way to the one Dani had been given. The one person who she had guessed had started the group Dani hoped she was about to meet and the one still helping after her death.

The key she needed.

"I'm Delacour's heir!" The last word stopped the wind whipping the chilly air, leaving a calm silence in its wake. That calm was swiftly broken by a giant sphere of what looked like molten metal dripping from the sky and landing only a few paces from where Dani was standing.

But while her security team pulled her back, the princess could only watch with wide eyes. The whirlpool that had just formed reminded her of the planetarium in Umbergrove, a sight too incredible to put into words. So she just stared down, only vaguely aware of Anders giving orders and pulling her farther back.

"Stop!" Dani hadn't realized she had been the one to speak the words until both bodyguards stared at her and scowled.

"You need to get to safety." Anders ordered, his tone leaving no room for her to argue. Dani did anyway.

"I think I'm supposed to let it take me," The idea clicked in her head and solidified. It felt much better than letting her protectors drag her away.

"Absolutely not," Libby shook her head. "As your bodyguard I am at complete liberty to say that jumping into a silver whirlpool is a very bad idea."

"What if I fall?" Dani forced herself closer to the ever growing whirlpool before her confidence ran out. She didn't relish being difficult to the two people assigned to protect her but she needed answers. Hopefully Anders and Libby could forgive her eventually.

"Don't even think about it!" Anders gave his most disapproving stare as he met her at the edge.

"I think she already has," Libby sighed. "Would it be helpful if I offered to freeze her toes before she moves any closer?"

Dani genuinely couldn't tell if she was joking.

Anders frowned. "I thought we discussed that the princess must trust us to protect her, not threaten her."

"Yes," Libby agreed hastily, "But our job is to keep her safe in all circumstances. Getting swallowed up by that thing does not seem safe."

Dani wanted to speak up in protest. She wanted to wave her arms and make them stop pretending that she didn't exist. But if she had learned one thing during her time on earth it was that sometimes being invisible came with an advantage.

Before her guards could attempt to stop her, Dani set her tiara down on the grass and jumped feet first into the shimmering whirlpool below.

Chapter Thirty-six

The ground Dani landed on was smoother than she had expected and didn't hurt her upon impact. Nor did it seem to hurt the two bodyguards that landed immediately afterwards.

Anders recovered first, and as soon as he helped her to her feet his face turned to stone. "Perhaps you didn't hear my warning a moment ago," There wasn't a hint of amusement on his face. "Or remember the many conversations we have had regarding safety protocols?"

"Well I didn't think you'd follow me," Dani mumbled back, averting her eyes downwards as Libby began to stand.

"As your bodyguards, that is our job." Anders replied evenly. If Dani had been in a safer situation she would have braced for a very long lecture.

"And as the savior this is mine." Dani kept her voice steady, bringing her gaze back up so she could face her head of security.

Her words didn't get much of a reaction from Libby but Dani knew deep down Anders had to understand. He had watched the mystery unfold from the start.

"You think this is where you are supposed to go," He didn't phrase the words as a question but Dani answered anyway.

"Yes," She said, her voice quiet but confident. "This has to be a hideout or a secret office or something." The room they were standing in was all stark silver, definitely not a normal sight for being underground.

"I don't think she's wrong on this one," Libby decided, pushing a blonde streak off of her shoulder. "Could this be part of a tunnel?" She ran a hand along one of the walls.

It definitely seemed like it could be.

"Perhaps," Anders agreed, stepping back to assess their sleek surroundings. "Though I don't see any switch that could reveal a door."

"They wouldn't lead me here just to trap me," Dani said, willing the words to be true.

"Do we even know who they are?" Libby brought up a frustratingly valid point.

Dani knew nothing about her supporters except that they were an organization that were now helping her per the former savior's request. She had no clue who the people were or how they had come to align with her ancestor.

"Other than the fact that they plan to save Dani's life, no." Anders answered for her. His tone was still even but Dani was perceptive enough to realize what he wasn't saying.

"This isn't a trap," Dani told them resolutely. "Maybe there's another way in?" She knelt down to check the floor for any loose pieces or trap doors. There were none.

"We could break the wall down," Libby suggested, and from the expression on her face it looked like she was ready and willing to do just that.

"Maybe I could just blast it?" It would drain all of her energy but Dani had destroyed small scale objects during her Thursday morning training session with Sir Hugo.

"That won't be necessary," The voice belonged to a shadowed figure in a long golden cloak who now stood before them. Dani wasn't sure how he had arrived.

"Unmask yourself!" Anders demanded, putting himself between Dani and the cloaked figure. Both he and Libby had their weapons raised.

If the brytlyn under the cloak was unnerved he didn't show it. "I apologize, Lieutenant Bower but for the sake of the savior's safety I cannot do that." The monotone voice was calm and precise.

"Me?" Dani pushed her way through the barricade to face the figure.

"Of course," A hint of amusement crept into the voice. "Who else would I be referring to?"

"I'm not sure," Dani said. "I haven't been given much of an explanation about your group."

"That will begin shortly, please follow me." The golden cloak walked over to the wall on Dani's left and placed a golden gloved hand on it. The wall parted on all sides.

Dani tried to follow but was promptly blocked by The Great Wall of Bodyguards.

"Stay behind me at all times," Anders made her swear it before he followed the cloaked figure down a wide silver hall and Dani walked behind him with Libby at her side, sword drawn.

"Are you allowed to answer questions?" Dani asked, awkwardly leaning to the side to see the golden cloak.

"Within reason, your highness."

"How many people are in your organization?" Dani asked, still trying to get a glimpse as they walked in their line. The hall was just as sleek as the holding room but didn't seem to have an end.

"Our organization has hundreds of members," The golden

cloak replied. "Today you will be meeting a select few."

"I will?"

"Yes, and in the future if they approve you will get to meet more."

Dani arched a brow. "Why would I need permission from them to meet more members?" Weren't they all there to help her?

"Because you will be meeting your council."

"Her council?" Libby spoke up before Dani could.

"The young savior is the new leader of The Golden Eagle. But since she has only just arrived a council has been leading in her place and will continue to assist her throughout this process."

The words shouldn't have shaken Dani to her core as much as they did. Her note and scroll had given her some context.

"I'm in charge of The Golden Eagle?" Dani hoped repeating the words would help herself accept them.

They didn't.

"The entire organization is yours," The golden cloak agreed.

The Ruby Savior

Chapter Thirty-seven

"You guys do realize that Dani is thirteen, right?" Libby narrowed her eyes at the shadowed face of the golden cloaked figure. "Not that she isn't capable or anything, but that's a lot of responsibility for a teenager."

"We are quite aware of her highness's age and capabilities." The golden cloak answered, just as collected as before he dropped the bombshell.

Dani was busy trying to get her brain to fit together the puzzle pieces within it. Her capabilities had never included being a good leader. That was way more geared towards the other Stallard twin, the one who would actually have to lead the realm.

Dani managed a smile when something solidified in her head. "So that's why my medallion is gold,"

"Everyone receives a similar one when they join our order. Consider it a welcoming gift from your council."

Her council.

"And when exactly will she be meeting this council?" Anders stopped walking and Dani had to move to the side to see the arched doorway in front of them.

"Right now!" An enthusiastic voice boomed the words and Dani sidestepped Anders to see its owner: a golden suit of armor.

"Please join us, we've been expecting you." The words weren't ominous but Anders still kept her behind him and raised his sword.

"The princess will be safe here," The suit of armor promised. "However, our conversation is private so all bodyguards must stay in the hall."

Dani felt bad for the suit of armor when both of her bodyguards argued at once. Very, very loudly and without mercy.

"My job is to protect the princess," Anders didn't move an inch and Libby looked like she would be making good on her threat to freeze someone very soon.

"And my job is to ensure the princess's safety while she is at our headquarters. I can assure you that no harm will come to her while she is with me and the rest of her council." The suit of armor seemed completely unfazed and didn't back down.

"You are part of my council?" Dani hadn't expected a suit of armor to advise her—or even to meet a suit of armor at all.

"You can call me Radian," the suit of armor said. Dani was trying to see if a brytlyn really was under there.

Libby crossed her arms, shooting a measuring glance at Radian. "Do you all use codenames?"

"It is for the princess's protection," A moving golden statue in a full metallic ball gown joined Radian. "It is a pleasure to have you here Danielle, my name is Nova."

"Your codename?" Dani guessed.

Nova nodded. "None of us are allowed to share our real names with you as an extra precaution."

"But you're all brytlyns, right?" The gold had to be there as another precaution.

"Yes," Dani didn't miss the hesitation in Nova's voice or the way Radian pretended not to hear it.

"Would I know any of you?" It was impossible to tell who was under the disguise but Dani still tried her best.

"No," Radian answered immediately. "But you will recognize a member of your council."

Dani hoped it wasn't Iris.

"We should begin introductions," Nova told him, ushering Dani into the room before Anders or Libby could stop her.

"She will be safe with us." She promised, waiting until Radian opened the door before shutting the door with Dani inside. And the weirdest part was that the princess actually believed her.

All the room contained was a horseshoe shaped table with three figures behind it. Two of them were dressed head to toe in gold disguises and the other was a brytlyn Dani recognized immediately and would never have suspected as a member.

She would've scrambled back had her advisors not been right behind her. "You're a part of The Golden Eagle?" Dani really wished Anders and Libby weren't in the hall.

It both made sense and was shocking all at once.

"Correct," Sir Hugo nodded calmly. "I have been leading in your absence."

Dani's eyebrows shot up to her hairline. "You knew Delacour?" Sir Hugo looked older than the other brytlyns Dani had met but she wouldn't have pegged him for over two hundred years old.

"There is a lot to be explained," The golden soldier to his left spoke up.

"But she is taking it better than what we anticipated." The

golden ballerina on Sir Hugo's right replied.

Nova and Radian left her near the door and made their way to stand behind the table as well, making the divide even more apparent. It was Dani against her council.

Her sparker instructor stood right in the middle of the council, eyes narrowed like he was trying to decide on how to proceed.

Dani was trying to decide whether or not to shout for her guards.

Her heart plummeted when another brytlyn entered and moved to stand beside the council.

"I thought we agreed that I would be the one to greet her, Hugo." The voice was just as heartbreakingly familiar as the person it belonged to.

Forget shouting and racing out the door, Dani was about to blast it apart and run.

"I stalled as long as I could but your daughter threatened to break down the wall herself and I do not doubt her capabilities in that department." Sir Hugo replied, sounding perfectly at ease while talking to the consort of the realm.

"You're a member of The Golden Eagle as well?" Dani backed herself up all the way to the wall and it still wasn't far enough.

It never would be.

"I am not an active operative but yes darling I am." Queen Amandine was still wearing her gown and tiara from the ball. On top of that she wore a long golden cloak.

The world could have exploded around Dani and she wouldn't have moved. Her hands itched to create a spark sphere out of the fear that seemed to consume her but she refrained. She needed to understand what was happening first.

Finding out the only other sparker alive was helping to lead her organization was hard enough to come to terms with and Dani barely knew him. She was grateful for his support and lessons of course, but he had only been with her two mornings a week for training.

Amandine had given birth to her.

"It was crucial that you figured this all out yourself before any interfering steps were taken. I did try to guide you as much as I could."

Callan had been overly protective since the news of her being the savior had broken but Amandine had been nothing but supportive. She hadn't even been angry about Dani hiding the scroll like Callan had. The truth became more and more apparent with every memory that ran through Dani's head.

"Were you the one who hid the book?" Dani stayed pressed against the wall even when her mother glided back around the table to move closer to her.

"I was, yes." She replied. "And the one who wrote in it."

The world spun around Dani, keeping her in the center of a dizzying whirlwind.

"I thought there was a security breach!" Dani cried, her voice working again. "Dad got me a security escort."

Amandine waited until Dani had calmed down before speaking. "If you remember, I was able to talk him into only adding Libby for the time being and you do seem to enjoy her company."

"Don't try to justify manipulating everything," Dani shot back. Her mother had been lying the entire time, orchestrating the entire plot.

"I'm not," Her mother promised calmly. "But I am trying to help you understand this as best I can before we must return to Elthorne."

"Where does dad think you are right now?" Dani was sure her father knew her whereabouts but there was no way Callan was aware of what his wife was a part of.

"Currently resting in our bedroom and feeling sick." Amandine answered, her otherwise passive expression betraying the slightest bit of guilt.

"What happens if someone tries to check on you?"

Her mom shrugged regally. "I didn't plan that far ahead, unfortunately. I had foolishly thought you wouldn't leave quite so early and hadn't been watching as you slipped away. Thank goodness I saw the Callisto boys and the Varron's returning with your brother or I never would have known."

"When do we have to go back because I'm going to need some answers first," Dani looked past her mother to the five council members still standing together.

"We can help with that," The golden ballerina said. "And you may call me Scala. What questions do you have?"

Dani had a long, long list.

"How long have you all known that I was the savior?" It had to have been before her arrival at the very least.

"We have known since your mother joined our order a few months after you were born," Sir Hugo's words did something to Dani's heart that made her turn completely away from her mother.

When Dani had found out that she was the savior everyone around her had panicked.

The Magicals had been confused.
Callan had been concerned.
Will had tried to learn everything he could.
Amandine had been lying.

"Did you know when I was born?" Dani turned to her mother, letting the sparks she had been holding back fly free.

Amandine shook her head only once. "No," She said, "I didn't know until after you were taken to earth."

Dani nodded, letting the information sink in. "When was this organization formed?" Delacour had become the savior at thirteen and died at eighteen, sometime in between The Golden Eagle had been created.

"This organization was formed shortly after the former savior defeated the rebels," Calling Delacour the former savior made Dani feel like a spotlight had been trained right on her. "It was formed by Princess Delacour to be more specific."

"How old was she?"

"Fifteen years old, though she hadn't heard the prophecy yet."

"She formed an organization at fifteen? How did she manage that?" Dani doubted she could do that.

Sir Hugo nodded carefully. "She saw that there were cracks in the realm and no one with a solution to fix them so along with some supporters Delacour formed The Golden Eagle and kept the peace even after her death."

"And had everything ready when I got old enough to take over," Dani realized, the puzzle pieces clicking into pieces.

Delacour had built a legacy away from the title she'd been born with. Dani was now poised to do the same.

"I'm really in charge of The Golden Eagle?" Saying the words out loud didn't help anymore than they had earlier when she had first learned the news.

"As of Delacour's final request, yes." Sir Hugo confirmed. "Though the choice is still yours whether or not to accept the responsibility."

Dani froze.
 "Choice?"
She hadn't known she had any choices.

"Your council has been keeping The Golden Eagle running for years. If you don't want to lead it you can simply say no and nothing will change on our end." Her mother explained, gaze steady. "The goal of this organization is to assist and guide you as best we can while working to prevent the end of the prophecy from occurring. That goal will not change regardless of your decision."

Sir Hugo nodded once Amandine had finished. "Your mother is correct, Dani. You have been the savior since even before you were born and that won't change. However, we all understand the enormity of the pressures you are facing and giving you another without your consent is cruel."

Radian set his hands on the table, armor clanking as he did so. "No matter what, your survival is what the group will be working towards each and every day until we prevail. So, our question is a simple yes or no, do you want to lead or not?"

Chapter Thirty-eight

"Could I have a minute?" Dani's head was spinning a million miles a minute and her sparks were swarming even faster.

Sir Hugo nodded. "Of course you can," He, her mother, and her council walked around the table and out the door Amandine had entered from.

Once she had been left alone Dani sat on the silver floor in silence, letting her spark sphere form and keep the world out.

She was well aware that the easy answer would be to tell her council that she wasn't ready to be their leader. Dani could have listed at least twenty dozen reasons why that was the right decision.

And she probably would have been leaning towards it if her sparks hadn't reminded her so much of the legacy Dani was now continuing.

Because the fight is bigger than I am.

It was true and Dani knew it.

If Breckindale would someday be in danger then there was no way that she would be able to save it all by herself and not die trying.

So when her council and Amandine entered back into the room a few minutes later Dani told them that she would lead their organization.

"You were brave to do that," Her mother led the way out of the tunnel half an hour later, not long after Dani had been briefed by her council of all the protocols she would need to know and follow.

"Thank you," Dani kept her tone even. Her mother had been lying to her for more than a week. She was still lying to Will and Callan. And the Magicals. And the realm.

"They showed you how to work your medallion, right?" Since Frost Crystals were so rare, The Golden Eagle had embedded tiny pieces of one into every member's medallion for blinking purposes. Instead of crushing it, all that was required for the blink was to either be in contact with the person holding the medallion or to be holding it yourself. Amandine was using hers to get them home but in the future Dani would use her personal one.

"Yeah, Nova explained it all to me." Anders and Libby had looked shocked when Dani had left the room with her mother at her side but hadn't uttered a single word not about their charge's safety in the moments since.

"I do hope you'll rely on your council, having advisors is invaluable to any leader." Her mother pulled out her medallion from her cloak pocket as she spoke, running her fingers over the engraved gold.

"But you've been lying to yours for years," Dani shot back, huddling close to Amandine only because it was necessary. She should have gone in between Libby and Anders.

A shadow crossed her mom's face, making it appear worn and tired. "Only when it was absolutely necessary,"

"And Callan and Will?" Dani was far from done with their conversation, even if her mother seemed finished speaking.

Both names creased Amandine's wrinkle free face. "This is not about the rest of our family, darling. They are not a part of this."

"So this only affects you and I?" Dani sucked in a breath while her mother sought an answer.

"For now, yes." Her mother's voice cracked for a moment before she cleared it and continued. "The Golden Eagle has to be kept secret for the safety of its members and you, even if that means not telling our family."

"Forever?"

"The rules can't change," Amandine's faraway gaze told Dani that her mother hated the rule just as much as she did.

Her mom didn't like lying either. She was just doing it to protect the organization Dani was now the sworn leader of.

Maybe Dani needed to start thinking like a leader, like a survivor.

Her mother gaze a sad smile. "I'm so sorry I had to lie and keep this from you, I truly am. And I am so incredibly proud of how you are handling this responsibility."

She gave one last glance before pressing the medallion's tip and blinking them all away from Frovland.

Dani had become quite adept at blinking since her arrival but this time she barely felt the rush of wind or saw the searing light as she landed right in Elthorne's courtyard flanked by her two bodyguards. Her mother was nowhere in sight.

"Well that was unexpected," Libby let out a strangled laugh, crossing her pink sleeved arms over her chest.

"Understatement of the year," Dani muttered as the guards posted at Elthorne's double doors let them into the palace. The music from the ballroom echoed through the foyer but Dani didn't follow its source.

"Research?" Anders watched as she climbed the stairs two at a time, shoes clacking against the marble once more.

"No," She called down. "Or not yet at least." None of the questions she had could be answered by books.

She wasn't the invisible girl anymore and she wouldn't be ever again. Breckindale's princess was the savior with a legacy left to her by a teenager who's fate had been tragic.

Dani's new goal was ensuring that hers wouldn't be.